MW00466223

TRUE 12 LOVE CHRISTMAS STORIES,

MY TRUE LOVE GAVE TO ME.

Ben Bongers, KM

En Route Books and Media, LLC

Saint Louis, MO

Make the time

En Route Books and Media, LLC
5705 Rhodes Avenue
St. Louis, MO 63109

Cover credit: Courtney Boatwright
Illustrated by Courtney Boatwright

ISBN-13: 978-1-956715-85-9 and 978-1-956715-87-3 and
978-1-956715-88-0
Library of Congress Control Number: 2022946659

Copyright © 2022 Ben Bongers
All rights reserved.

No part of this booklet may be reproduced, stored in a re-
trieval system, or transmitted in any form, or by any means,
electronic, mechanical, photocopying, or otherwise, without the prior written permission of the author.

To Lisa.

You are the sole reason for these 12 fancies.
With all my care, joy, and adoration.
I love you.

On the _____ day of Christmas...

(Foreword)

In the Summer of 2022, I went out to lunch with my publisher. I was still flying high (and exhausted) from getting my first book, *The Saint Nicholas Society*, published. It hadn't even been out a month when he asked me at lunch, "So, what's your next one?" After pretending to take my time chewing so I could think, I heard my wife's voice in my head nagging...I mean encouraging me...to publish some of the short stories I'd written for her.

Back when we were first married, budgets were tight. My wife and I agreed that at least one gift had to be found or "pre-used" (a.k.a. from a thrift store), and the Advent gifts had to be made or crafted. We always celebrated Advent, so, my first "crafted" gift was a 5- or 6-page creation entitled *A Partridge in a Pear Tree*. I would give her a page a week until I gave her the last 3 on Christmas Eve. She immediately put all the pages together and gave the story its first a full read through. By June, she was already asking (weekly) what the next story was going to be, hinting strongly, it *had* to be about two turtledoves! These requests quickly turning into a 12-year labor of love.

(A side note—the 12 days of Christmas are supposed to be celebrated *after* Christmas, not before. And yes, it annoys me when they stop playing the Christmas carols on the radio on December 26th! But that is my own pet peeve!)

The 12 Days of Christmas song was originally written for the Christian Faithful, to help people keep track of their catechism. But I didn't want to retell those stories. No. They've been done. I wanted to take a different twist. Loosely keeping the verse's words, but spinning a new story evoking real emotion, showing a human arch, then bringing back the verse's theme at the end—tying all together with a bit of a moral.

To give myself another challenge (why make it easy?), I also thought I would use the Boy Scout Laws as a loose pairing. I was a Boy Scout (shout out to Troop 283 Raytown, MO) and on staff at the local Scout Reservation, as well as an Eagle Scout—so the Boy Scout Laws were drilled into me—just like my catechism.

Here's how the verses and Laws line up: *A partridge in a pear tree*—Trustworthy, *Two turtledoves*—Loyal, *Three French Hens*—Helpful, *Four calling/Colly birds*—Friendly, *Five golden rings*—Courteous, *Six geese a laying*—Kind, *Seven swans a swimming*—Obedient, *Eight maids a milking*—Cheerful, *Nine ladies dancing*—Thrifty, *Ten lords a leaping*—Brave, *Eleven pipers piping*—Clean, *Twelve drummers drumming*—Reverent.

So, back to that lunch… I swallowed, took a breath and said, "I have a retelling of *The 12 Days of Christmas*. Actually, they're a twist and departure from the title of each verse." I immediately thought, "That's it. I'll never be heard from again…" Instead, the publisher leaned in and asked me to tell him the stories! After I went through 4 or 5, he said, "That's it. I want those. Those are your next book. Do you think you can get it to me by mid-September for this Christmas?"

So, here we are.

This book comes with a huge WARNING! Stamped on it!

Let's face it, life is messy and so are emotions. But, as Hellen Keller said, "The best and most beautiful things in the world cannot be seen or even touched. They must be felt with the heart."

This book was written with love, for someone I love, and who loves me in return. These twelve stories contain every emotion that we feel daily, but we're too afraid to let out. They are offered in the hope that readers will give themselves permission to really feel. To laugh, to hope, and yes… to cry. What better time of life than the Holidays to open that little door to our hearts that we slam shut and lock most of the time.

As was written down many, many years ago in Ecclesiastes, there's "a time to weep, and a time to laugh; a time to mourn, and a time to dance..." I hope these stories let you find a few minutes to pause and remember everything this season means.

—Ben

My true love gave to me...

(Acknowledgments)

These stories were explicitly scribbled for Lisa Anderson Bongers for Advent gifts over twelve plus years. Thank you for continually being my inspiration on every good thing I've created, done, and completed in my life. Without your constant love, support, and "what if you..." comments, I'd still be trying to figure out the difference between a noun and a verb. Thank you for being my muse.

I also must thank the wonderful friends, testers, and sounding boards that have read through these chapters, giving "what ifs," then double, triple and quadruple checking my facts, storylines, and content. You have my admiration and awe. It's not an easy thing to take someone else's work and feel safe enough to make open and honest comments. It's a true tribute to trust and honesty. Thank you.

Namely, I'd like to thank—Mrs. Linda Ade Brand, Bob Brand, and Julia Brand for your openness, sense of theater, and feedback on what works, and what *really* works. I owe you a few boxes of tissue. Ms. Karen Klein Elsloo, for the wonderful insights, inspiration, and motivation. Mr. Erik

Christianson, EdD, whose constant friendship and soul-filling comments helped keep the right direction in all of the stories. Mr. Timothy Pursell, PhD, a master of asking questions to flesh out, keep historical accuracy, and find depth of spirit in these stories. Ms. Laurel Ann Winzler, for keeping the nuts and bolts of all aspects of the stories on the right track. Ms. Mary Orth, for asking the questions that ground every character. And most especially to Noel Fulkerson, musician, parson, and mentor. You have known me and guided me for many, many years, and understand the hope, care, and inspiration that a single piece (be it musical or written word) can bring to a soul. Thank you for your guidance and comments one and all.

A very special thank you must go out to two special people. First, Courtney Boatwright, artist extraordinaire! Your exquisite art for each chapter completely encapsulates the spirit and story in a single picture. Second, Dr. Sebastian Mahfood OP and all at En Route Books and Media LLC, for being an extraordinary support base and nurturing spirit of talent. You have my undying gratitude and friendship.

And last, but in no ways least, you, dear reader! Without your picking up this book of stories, no one would ever see, and step into the wildings of my imagination!

Thank you and be well!

—Ben

Table of Contents

I

A PARTRIDGE IN A PEAR TREE

A Partridge in a Pear Tree

"...*and a Partridge in a pear tree!*" wafted out the door as only second-graders could sing it. The fourteen children were led by the ever-smiling Sister Mary Jo. She was in her element and adored everything Christmas. She had seen fifty-four Christmases come and go, thirty of them with the Sisters of the Sacred Heart and was still as excited as her second graders when she saw the first snowflake fall outside the windows of their south Chicago orphanage.

"Ssisster," lisped a little girl, two front teeth missing and with big doe eyes while tugging on the nun's habit. "Ssisster, why is there a partridge in the pear tree in the song?"

Sister Mary Jo pointed her finger up to the sky, then swooped it to her lips. The giggling children followed her lead and held a finger to their mouths and fell silent, as they'd been trained to do.

"If you sit in a circle, I'll tell you a little story about 'The Partridge in an Old Pear Tree,' just like that one out there." She pointed at an aging pear tree outside the classroom window.

The children loved Sister Mary Jo's stories and clamored for them at least once a day. She would weave tales out of thin air, always with a little twinkle and twist, tailoring them to match a weekly theme that would be on a bulletin board by the old oak door. The fables would make everyone feel special and wanted. This was a real need for every child in the class since each had been abandoned in some way. This week the word was "TRUSTWORTHY."

She moved to the window where the snow quietly fell and looked out at the leafless pear tree as the children sat in a semi-circle at her feet. "Many years ago, in a country far, far away there was a very good man. He was a cobbler. Now," she turned to the class and asked, "who can tell me what a cobbler is?"

Hands shot up around the room in a flurry, followed by, "O sister... Pick me... Oh... Oh... Me, me, me!"

The smiling nun looked over the children, but her eyes fell on the newest child in the orphanage, Jillian. Neither Jillian's hand, eyes, nor head were raised. She was staring down into her lap and hadn't uttered a word in the two days since she came to live at the school.

"Oh, Sister, a cobbler's a man who sells *corn* on the corner to all the rich peoples that walks by!" said one little boy, very proud of his answer.

"Nah... No way! Nuh, uh..." were the replies.

"Bong! You lose!" and "Whatcha been smokin'?" were a few others.

Sister Mary Jo smiled, still looking at Jillian, and offered a silent prayer. *Lord, show me how to help Jillian. She's a lost sheep in need of a shepherd.* The nun turned her attention to the little boy who gave the answer and gently corrected, "No, Bobby, I said coB-BL-er, not co-B-B-B-er. He doesn't have a lot of corn cobs lying around."

Sister Mary Jo's eyes got big as she looked around the room, "Now, who makes *shoes*?" she prompted.

All the hands went up. All but Jillian's. Trying to draw her into the family, Sister Mary Jo called, "Jillian, do you know who makes shoes?"

Jillian looked up for the first time with big moist eyes. She'd obviously been daydreaming of better times with people she'd known since birth. Staring at Sister Mary Jo for a few seconds, Jillian lightly shook her head and looked back at her lap.

"Jillian my angel, do you know who makes shoes?" asked Sister Mary Jo, trying to steady her own voice.

Still looking at her lap, Jillian answered, "A ca... ca...cobbler?"

"That's right! A *star* for my newest little angel!"

The entire class rallied around Jillian's answer with "Yay! Way to go Jillian! Awesome!" Jillian gave a brief smile before her eyes again fell to her lap. She was on her way to being a part of the family of Saint Anthony's orphanage.

"Well, my angels," started Sister Mary Jo, quickly conjuring a tailor-made story to fit her classes needs. "There once was a cobbler who made wooden shoes."

"Wooden shoes?" rioted the class.

"Who would ever wear wooden shoes?"

"Wouldn't they give you splinters?"

"No way Sister! You telling us fibs!"

"Oh, oh, oh my angels! In other countries and other times, people used to wear many different things than we do today. Now, this cobbler was an old, poor, and bent-over man who needed wood to make the new king in his country a pair of his famous shoes for the king's first feast."

"Sister?" asked a girl in the back with her hand waving above her head. "What's a feast?"

"A feast? Oh, that's a *big* party with foods and drinks from all over the world! There are cookies and punches and candies and tacos from every taqueria!"

"Can *we* have a feast sister? Can we huh? Yes! Please, can we?" came the questions spilling from around the room.

"We'll see." Sister Mary Jo scowled comically at the class and raised an outstretched finger to them. "It will depend on your next spelling test."

Becoming soft again, she went on. "Now, the old cobbler needed wood from an old tree that was treated with love and kindness. He knew where such trees grew in the Great Forest. But he didn't have enough time to go that far, because it was many, many days journey, and the feast was only a week away!"

"What did he do? Where did he go? How did he do it?" came the questions from the spell-bound youngsters.

Sister Mary Jo smiled and caught Jillian's glance. Her head was still down, but her eyes were up, and she was listening to the story very intently.

"Well," Sister Mary Jo began to pace back and forth before her class, her hands behind her back, "the cobbler was *very* upset. He would be the only person in the village who would not have a *special gift* to give to the new king. The cobbler moved around the house all day crying out, "What will I do? What will I do? I have no time; I have no money; I have no wood to make new shoes for the king…"

"We can help him sister! We can take up a colla… a colli… a… collection for him!" Came an answer from the class.

"Well now, that's very sweet of you dears! We must *always* help those who need it, but the cobbler already had help on the way!" Sister Mary Jo reached behind her and wrapped on the window behind her. "The cobbler heard a little knocking on the windowpane and saw it was a tiny partridge sitting on his windowsill."

"No way! Cool! I saw a partridge once!" came the squeals.

"He opened it and the little bird bowed and introduced himself as Alphonse P. Partridge. He told the cobbler, "No more worries! Help is on the way. You will have your wood soon! And remember, when you really need help, God will provide! Trust in the Lord" With that Alphonse P. Partridge flew up into the pear tree just outside the cobbler's house.

"So, what happened? Why did he go? What happened next?" quizzed the class.

"The next day, the cobbler was even *more* worried than the first and paced back and forth. 'Oh, what will I do? I cannot go to the Great Forest, and I do not have the money to buy the wood I need! Oh, I will not have anything for the new king for his feast.' Again, the cobbler heard a knocking at the window. And again, Alphonse P. Partridge bobbed his head in the window frame. 'Do not worry my dear cobbler. Help is on the way. You'll have your wood *very* soon. Please try to remember, when you really need help…'"

Sister Mary Jo put her hand out, prompting the children. They all yelled in one voice, "God will provide!"

"And… Trust?" Sister Mary Jo circled her right hand to the class.

"Trust in the Lord!" yelled the class.

"That's right! Because God is *trust worthy*, He is deserving of our trust. Very good my little angels!"

"So, what happened?" asked Jillian, in a very small voice, head now up and facing Sister Mary Jo.

The nun had a grin on her face, uttering a short, "Thank you," to heaven.

Sister Mary Jo began to move around the room, almost dancing. "Well, every day for the next three days the same thing happened. The cobbler would worry, and stew, and Alphonse P. Partridge would come, rap on the windowpane, and say, 'Do not worry my dear cobbler. Help is on the way.

Trust in the Lord!' Finally, a *great storm* came to the small village. Thunder *BOOMED* and lightning *FLASHED*, and the cobbler was very frightened for his life."

The nun stopped and crouched down with her students. "Have you ever been scared during a storm?"

"Oh yes, Sister!"

"Me? Nah…"

"They don't scare me none!" came responses with abandon.

"Well, they scare me something terribly!" admitted Sister Mary Jo. "In fact, when I hear that thunder or see lightning flash, I say a little prayer. I say, "No matter what, I will be fine because…"

Again, Sister Mary Jo put out a hand prompting the youngsters, and they yelled back, "God will provide! Trust in the Lord!"

"That's right, God is trustworthy, and He will *always* provide.

"Now, that night, as the storm raged on, the cobbler heard a great *crack* and a big *boom* outside the window. The cobbler was too scared to look outside the window and fell down to the floor, then crawled under his bed until morning! When he woke, he went out and noticed the old pear tree had been hit by lightning! It broke in *half*, just outside his window."

The children began to holler and whoop! "Alphonse P. Partridge was right! It came true! Oh wow!"

"And do you know what the cobbler did then?" asked Sister Mary Jo.

"Yeah! Now he can make his shoes! Wow! He got it after all..."

"That's right children, very good! You figured it out!" Sister Mary Jo said, as she clapped her hands together. She caught a quick glimpse of Jillian out of the corner of her eye.

Jillian quietly and sheepishly lifted her little hand.

"Yes Jillian, you have a question?"

"Sister? What happened to Alphonse?"

Sister Mary Jo froze for a moment and silently prayed the little prayer when she didn't know where her stories would go next. *Holy Spirit, guide me.*

Her prayer was quickly answered with words that popped out of her mouth before she thought. "Well, Jillian, the cobbler looked for him, but found him lying next to the tree. Dead."

Sister Mary Jo couldn't believe the words that came out of her mouth! *Why* did she say that? *Why* did the story take this very dark path? What was happening?

Jillian looked down, then back up at Sister Mary Jo hesitantly asking, "Was Alphonse P. Partridge an angel?"

Sister Mary Jo gave a relieved smiled. "Maybe, my little angel, maybe..."

Big tears formed and hung in Jillian eyes. "My mommy and daddy died in a big storm. The one we had two weeks ago. They were driving back from a party— a, a feast—and a big tree fell on their car, and…"

Sister Mary Jo was dumbfounded. She didn't know what to say as a chill ran down her spine.

Jillian smiled as the two giant tears spilled out and down her cheeks, "Maybe my mommy and daddy *saw* Alphonse before they died." Jillian voice had hope in it.

Sister Mary Jo went to Jillian, wrapped her arms around her, held her close, whispering in her ear, "I'm sure they did my angel, I'm sure they did…"

▶◆◆◆◀

Twenty years later

Seventeen raucous second graders sang the line, "*… and a Partridge in a pear tree!*" The sound came wafting out as a new teacher walked down the hall at Sacred Heart School in South Chicago. It was her first day and she was a bundle of nerves carrying her new briefcase. This was her first assignment after receiving a teaching degree and taking her final vows only weeks earlier. The newest member of the Sisters of the Sacred Heart stopped at the door for a moment before entering with an older nun at her elbow.

"Children," said Sister Mary Jo, now principal of the school. "I would like to introduce you to your *new* teacher, Sister Mary Jillian." She moved into the room and looked back at the new nun in the doorway. "She was a student in this very room many, many years ago!"

"Wow! How old are you?"

"Do you like kids?"

"Why did you go to school here?" came the endless inquiries.

"Now children, let Sister Mary Jillian settle in before you start with all the questions."

Sister Mary Jo turned to Sister Mary Jillian and said quietly, "If you need me, I'll be down the hall," and gave Sister Mary Jillian a quick hug then scurried out of the room.

Sister Mary Jillian sat her briefcase down by the desk and took off her coat, hanging it on the nearby hook. She rubbed her fear-chilled hands together and felt a little finger poking her thigh. "Scuse me... Scuse me... Do you like our singing?"

"Your singing? Why, yes! Yes, I do! It was lovely."

"Thank you, Sister! Awesome! Cool!" chortled the room.

"Sister?"

"Yes?"

"Do you know the partridge in a pear tree song?"

"Yes, um, what's your name, sweetheart?" asked Sister Mary Jillian.

"I'm Kenisha," said a little girl with a big smile and two front teeth missing.

"Yes, Kenisha, I do know the partridge in the pear tree song."

Sister Mary Jillian moved toward the window and held her hands over the heat register. The last time she'd been in this room she was a new second grade student, and Sister Mary Jo was the teacher. How would she ever fill those shoes?"

"Sister, Sister… Why is there a partridge in the pear tree in the song?"

Sister Mary Jillian heard the question echo in her mind's ear. She looked out the window at the old pear tree that still stood outside. It was covered in snow and looked lifeless. But she knew that in the spring, it would sprout leaves and bloom back to life, much as she had in this very room all those years ago.

Then, as if in a dream, something unexpected happened. A bird. A simple bird landed on the limb that brushed the classroom window and tapped the window three times with its tiny beak.

"Why, it's a…" Sister Mary Jillian breathed.

"What kinda bird is that?" asked a little boy in the class.

"It's… It's a partridge!" she said before turning around to face the class, and a new life.

"God will provide. Trust in the Lord…" she whispered and wiped away a single tear.

"Well, my little angels… Do any of you know what a cobbler is?"

TWO TURTLE DOVES

Two Turtledoves

Found in: **"Art Extraordinaire Magazine"** – *June edition.*
Interview conducted by Jennifer Newcomb.

The following interview took place in Pueblo, Colorado at 'Misfit Toys Studio,' the home workspace of Belanima Chavez. Ms. Chavez, who now goes simply by the name Belanima, is a tour de force in the art world, with descriptors like "depth," "pathos," and "humor" as trademarks. Her sculptural works in glass and wood have been shown in many A-list museums like the Museum of Modern Art (MOMA) in New York and the de Young in San Francisco. She had a one woman showing last year at the Paris Museum of Modern Art that was filled with wood, metal and plastics, exploring color and form. And she will be co-opening a new exhibition with a retrospective of Christo at the Tate in London later this year.

Art Extraordinary Magazine was privileged to speak with her in her studio while she worked on a new small-scale piece.

Art Extraordinary Magazine: Thank you Belanima for speaking with us today. Tell me Belanima, what are you working on?

Belanima: *(Belanima holds up a 2'x3' piece of raw wood)* It's a piece of Basswood I cut down myself the last time I was in a French Pyrenees Forest, about three years ago. The trees there are grown in little protective pockets in the mountain valleys and don't have a lot of wind blowing them around. So, the grain is tight and perfectly straight. I carved the bigger piece of this into the thirteen faced, 'American Totem' for the Smithsonian exhibition last fall.

AEM: You're known for storytelling through solid media like wood, metal, and glass. What is this project you're working on, and what was its inspiration?

B: Well, usually I plan a project out by doing a bunch of research, just to get to know the culture and flow of the subject matter. Then I'll make far too many sketches and determine what the medium will be that I want to birth a piece out of. But this one, well... it's different. I had a dream about this project last week. I love to work with wood in particular. It's the medium I first felt comfortable in.

AEM: Where did your artistic spark come from? Your mother or father?

B: *(laughing)* Oh no! I'm exactly the opposite of my mother. She's this prissy, 1950s, June Cleaver kind of woman that

enjoys knitting tea cozies in her spare time. Hey! There's
nothing wrong with that but... that's definitely not me.
She knows how I feel and she's okay with that. We can't
all be the same. No, I'm much more like my Nona, my
grandma. She was a 'Rosie the Riveter' in World War II
and raised a family of five for three years without a husband because of the war. She was not only a great inspiration to me but also, well, my best friend.

AEM: You've said in the past your grandmother has been a
large influence on your career.

B: Yes, for as long as I can remember. She and I were thick
as thieves. I remember when Billy Romberg, a complete
and utter ass-hat bully, and yes—I hope he reads this—
used to pester me every day in the third grade. My
mother sat me down and said I had to simply avoid him.
I didn't understand what that meant at the time but, I
was a good daughter and tried to follow her advice because, you know... she was my mother. My Nona just sat
there and rolled her eyes. I could always tell when she
didn't agree with my mother. She'd just look at me and
her eyes would make this large circle. It would always
crack me up. She'd just go back to reading the paper, or
sculpting, or whatever it was she was doing. Nona was
always there for me. Even when I screwed up or when I
was headed in the wrong direction. No, check that. Not
the wrong direction, as she'd say, 'I just wasn't taking the
path that I was meant to take at the time.' She's always

been loyal to me and guided me back to the right road—my road.

AEM: In all of my research, I've never heard anything about your father. Was he a force in your life?

B: No, not really. I mean, I know I HAVE a father but, that's more of a biological knowledge, not a practical one. He was never really around when I was young. He was always at work. And then one day—I must have been five or six—he went away on a business trip and never came home.

AEM: And how did that affect you and your family?

B: It didn't. Not really. I mean, well, maybe. I really didn't know him that well. I don't have ANY real memories WITH him, or OF him from my young life so, I can't really be traumatized by something I've never known, can I?

(A mourning dove landed in a windowsill and cooed, pecking at the window. Belanima put her tools down to watch.)

B: That mourning dove reminds me of my mom and Nona. My Nona and I were thick as thieves. I can still hear Mom calling us her, "two turtledoves," because we were always whispering back and forth. She'd yelp at us, 'What are you two turtledoves doing in there?' Or, if we were giggling at church or in a restaurant, she'd lean over to us in a loud whisper, 'Will you two turtledoves stop cooing?

People are staring!' My mom was really irritated at times but, she was right. We're inseparable in spirit and mind. My grandmother knows what I'm thinking and what I'm going to do before I do it. Heck, she *is* an older me! I sure hope I'll be like her when I grow up!"

AEM: Is she an artist as well?

B: Nona? She's an amazing artist. She would sculpt, render, and paint all the time. She especially loved wood, pencil work, and oil paint. She only did one show, but she had a family to take care of and, well, like so many others, everyone else's needs came first. I think that's where I got my talent. No, I KNOW that's where I got my talent. She was my inspiration, then and now. Anytime I had a drawing to make, or a watercolor to paint, or later, a major sculpture to formulate—I would go to her. She has the best ideas out of anybody I know. She would've been a great artist in her own right, if she had the time and backing, like she gave me.

(Belanima searched around the shop for a time).

B: "Oh, would you do me a favor? Would you hand me that gouge over there? Thank you.

AEM: How would you describe to someone how you bring your work to life?

B: Well, take this plaque I'm working on. If I gouge here, like this, and take a chip here... here... and here... you begin to see the swoops and twirls more clearly. They become present. Even though it's solid wood, what you see has movement, draping and sheen.

AEM: You mentioned your grandmother was an inspiration. Outside of art, in what ways?

B: Oh, so many... She really helped me when it came time to figure out what I wanted to do with my life. When I was seventeen and all my friends were going away to college and getting married, and stuff like that. Well, I wasn't interested in any of it. I mean, I was dating a nice person and all but, I didn't see me *marrying* them and settling down and having twenty-seven kids and all that, like my mom did. Well, mom didn't have twenty-seven kids but... You get the idea. I wanted to travel and do the things I wanted to do. All I knew was my favorite class in school was Shop, and all I wanted to do was design things.

AEM: Let's dive a little deeper. How did your grandmother influence you?

B: Well, after going out with some friends, I'd had it. I didn't fit in, I was all alone, even though I was in a car full of people, I felt like everything I did was wrong. I could SEE things that were obvious to me—color, movement, art all around us—but the people I was hanging with didn't see any of it and would make fun of me. So, I just shut down. I didn't talk. Instead, to get by, I got numb. I'd drink, do lightweight drugs, anything to take the edge off.

One night, June first, I was seventeen, I'll never forget it as long as I live... I came in, I'm sure reeking of weed, and went straight to Nona's room. I knocked, went in, and crawled into bed with her, bursting into tears. She hugged me close and didn't say a word for the longest time. No, 'Where have you been?' No, 'Why do you smell like a bar?' No, 'What have you been smoking?' Nothing. Once I calmed down, I told her that I didn't know what I wanted to do. That I didn't fit in and didn't have a clue as to what I was expected to do. She said, 'Baloney!' Well, actually, she said it using different words than that, but... She said I'd known for years but was too scared to go after it. I swear, I didn't have a clue as to what I wanted to do. But, within ten minutes, she helped me see what I'd been preparing for all my life. I was going to be a designer, and craftsperson! I owe it all to her. No matter what scrape or scuffle I was in, she was always there. Just like an old hound dog—loyal to the end.

(She sanded for a bit, then began to dig deeply into the rough and chopped up block of basswood. Two forms emerged from the thin-grained, light-colored wood.).

AEM: And your mother? What influence has she had on you or your art?

B: None really. I don't mean that in a callus or mean way. I really don't. It's just, well... I feel you have to be close; I mean really close to someone before you really feel an influence—positive *or* negative. The people who have really had an influence on me have been other artists, Chihuly, Matisse, Ben Butler... people like that. In my personal life, I have a couple friends that know way too much about me from like first grade, and my grandmother. Again, don't get me wrong, I love my mother. But we really don't have the same... Hmm... the same language as other artists or my Nona have.

AEM: So, after your time at university and traveling Europe, how did you land back here, in Colorado and your old neighborhood?

B: I've always loved designing and carving and sculpting and creating... no matter where I am. But there's always an unsettledness to the process for me in other places. A sort of ungroundedness. I needed to be where I was known, really known by someone and, that's my Nona. She inspires me and stands by me in rough times, and celebrates, not just my art, but who I really am. To make a long story short, I'm doing *what* I have to, *where* I have to, and *when* I have to.

AEM: Your art is unique and recognizable. Has it always been that way? How did you find your artistic voice?

B: Oh no... *(laughing)* No, no, no, no, no! No, my first four or five years were pretty lean and unfocused. I was trying a little bit of this and that and not really honing-in on any one style. And again, Nona came to the rescue. I was feeling like I was a failure. Nothing I made was getting any recognition or selling. I know she didn't want me to know it but, I found out later. I found out my grandma bought my first four years' worth of woodworking pieces, then gave them to friends of hers. She backed me and helped get me self-confidence, and I didn't even know it! I just found out a few months ago, and I'd love to have them back! Seriously, they were so bad! (laughing) I mean it! They were awful! But Nona stood by me through thick and thin. She saw to it that I stuck to my dream. Yup. She's the only one who believed in me. I'm sorry, I'm just rambling here…

AEM: Your grandmother really seems to be the biggest influence in your career.

B: Not just my career, my life! Here, you asked earlier what I'm working on. Well here, take a look. It's a two, by three, plaque of a pair of birds sitting in their nest. I had a very weird dream one night last week, and well, it just seemed more important to work on this than the projects for the Tate. It's sort of funny. With every gouge, every cut, every dig… I thought about my Nona. Kind of weird, isn't it? I'm sorry. I kept talking about my Nona all the way through this interview. It's just… Well, she's on my mind a lot today.

(Belanima inspected the piece, then retrieved a fine grade awl and scratched her moniker into the lower right corner).

B: There. Finished.

AEM: Do you have a home for this piece picked out?

B: I do! After our little chat today, I think I'll give it to my Nona. She's stood behind me and supported me all these years. It's about time for me to give her something of quality in return.

▶◆◆◆◀

A postscript to the earlier interview with Belanima.

Two weeks after this interview *Art Extraordinary Magazine* received a handwritten note from Belanima. We received permission to print it here:

During my recent interview with *Art Extraordinary Magazine,* the question was asked if I had "a home" for the piece I was working on. It was a bas-relief of two doves in a nest together. I don't know where the inspiration came from, and I don't know why I had such a drive to finish it.

And, as you remember, during the interview a mourning dove flew in and sat on the windowsill, overlooking where I work. At the end of the interview, I said that I thought it was about time to give my Nona a work of mine to thank her for all the years she's been there for me.

Twenty minutes after the interview ended, my mother called and told me my Nona had passed. The strange and beautiful part is, she was passing at the exact time the mourning dove came to visit.

Even though I didn't tell her enough, I hope she realizes what an inspiration she was, and how much she meant to me. I thought you would like to know that the piece became my farewell gift to my Nona. It was with her when she was buried. It was placed over the top of her casket, so she'll always remember her little turtledove.

Never neglect telling those close, "I love you."

—Belanima

THREE FRENCH HENS

Three French Hens

A blanket of stars twinkled and shone in the night sky over the picturesque town of Saverne, nestled deep in the Alsace of France. As the clock tower in the church square struck eleven, three girls cried out entering the world, becoming the newest citizens of the village. Three different midwives in three different houses offered three little red-faced souls to their fathers, asking the same question, "What shall be her name?"

Almost in unison, they each answered,

"Henrietta."

"Henrietta."

"Henrietta."

Thus, the three French Hens were born; their names written down with the month and day in the big book marked 1927 at City Hall.

Henrietta Pompeux's family had been a part of the fabric of Saverne for over a thousand years. Knights, wine makers and bankers made up the trunk of the family tree. Henrietta's mother and father, Henri and Mathilde, had hoped, had prayed for fourteen years to receive the child nature now supplied. The couple doted and fussed over the little girl as if she were a golden treasure, and she had puppies and ponies to keep her company.

On her fifth birthday, Henrietta walked over the freshly washed cobble street with her father, passing the Hôtel de Ville and other offices to the Poney D'Or Brasserie for his favorites, escargot, goose pâté, and frog's legs. Henrietta didn't much like the taste of the food, but she liked making her father happy, and she got to pick her favorite desert— raspberry torte. On the way out of the brasserie, she noticed a man with torn pants, his back to a building, sitting, and rubbing a sockless foot. "Daddy, why do we have so much, and others in the village have so little? Is it right that we have so much?"

Henri smoothed his long mustache with his gloved hand and looked at her for a moment. "Henrietta, remember one thing. Being poor is a terrible, terrible thing. It brings disease and pestilence. People who are poor deserve being poor. They are lazy and don't have breeding like you or your mother. Therefore, they are not as *good* as you and I. These are people to stay away from. Do you understand? You must choose your friends carefully. Only the best."

Henrietta looked up at Henri with big pure blue eyes, not fully understanding the words her father spoke. But, when her father smiled at her and said, "Understand?" she vigorously nodded her head. She liked to please her Papa.

On the other side of the city park was a smallish, shabby three-story house with five older girls hanging laundry on a line at the back. Henrietta Abram was standing next to her papa's reading chair while her father, Isaac, chided her. "Men don't want a dumb nudnik following them to temple! They need brains for figures, for measuring, for rearing children. You should need to settle down to what is important. You will never find a man who will light your birthday cake should you not!"

"But Papa, I'm only five. I have no need for a husband as yet."

"Nonsense! Women are born for husbands, just ask your mother."

Henrietta turned her head, seeing her mother enter the dining room with a small birthday cake and five glowing candles on it, followed by her five sisters. "Mama, do I need a husband?"

Golda smiled and giggled slightly, "What?" She caught a glimpse of the scowl on Isaac's face and her head quickly drooped along with her smile. "My dear Henrietta, you must always listen to your father. Now, we should have some cake before the wax melts."

Across the park and over the small stream lay the oldest house in town. "*This home was built by Helmut L'utile with care in the year of our Lord 1400,*" was carved over the front door of the house that leaned a bit, needing some loving care.

Etienne L'utile sat next to his daughter in their favorite spot, on the bank of the stream under a weeping willow. His white shirt sleeves and pantlegs were rolled up, both their feet dangling in the cold stream.

"Oh, my little Hen, I wish your mother were here to see how you've grown." He ran his fingers through her flaxen hair as she leaned into him, laying her head on his chest. "Here you are, five years old, and as beautiful as your mamma."

"Papa, tell me a story about her."

"All right…" he thought, tossing a leaf into the gentle current. "A week before you came, and before…" Etienne felt his throat tighten, his eyes becoming misty. He took a deep breath to check his emotions."…and before she left us, we came down here and sat in this very spot, your mother and I."

"You did?"

"Yes, my little Hen, we did." He wrapped his arm around her, drawing her in close, smelling her hair. "She was full of life. We sat, just like this, my arm around her, her head on my chest, and just sat.

"Just sat?"

"Mm-hm…" he smiled at the memory. "We just sat and talked about how wonderful our…" he cleared his throat again, this time a tear freed itself from the crease of his right eye. "How wonderful our life was going to be with you in it. The things we would do, the places we'd see, the dreams we'd have." Etienne hugged Henrietta even closer, and she snuggled into him in the quiet.

After seeing a turtle glide by in the stream, Etienne kissed her on the top of the head, and asked, "And then do you know what we did?"

"No Papa, what?"

"We skipped stones across the stream." Etienne sprang up from the place they sat and looked for a few small flat stones on the bank.

"Did she throw well?"

Etienne smiled, "No, she didn't. But it didn't matter. She was always smiling, and cheerful, and helped anyone who needed it." He looked down at his daughter and hugged her close. "Just like you."

"Papa?"

"Yes?"

"Can you show me how to skip a stone on the water?"

"Yes, my little Hen…"

Later, on their birthday afternoon, all three girls found their ways to the park—Henrietta Pompeux with her new nanny, Henrietta Abram with her oldest sister, and Henrietta L'utile by herself, as her father was trying to find work at the local mill. Soon, the nanny moved to the far corner of the park where the other nannies were chatting and knitting, and Henrietta Abram's older sister abandoned her to go shopping with some friends.

"Hello," said Henrietta Abram to Henrietta Pompeux, "I like your dress. It's very pretty."

"Thank you," said Henrietta Pompeux to Henrietta Abram. "My Papa bought it for me today before we went to lunch." Henrietta Pompeux looked at Henrietta Abram's dress and asked, "Where did your father buy your dress?"

Henrietta Abram giggled, "My Papa didn't buy my dress silly, he made it! He's a tailor."

From across the park, a blue ball with pink circles bounced to where the two girls stood. Henrietta L'utile ran to the two, and said, "My Papa gave me this ball, cause today's my birthday! Would you like to play with me?"

"Mine too!" said, Henrietta Abram.

And it's my birthday, too!" said Henrietta Pompeux.

The three began to kick, throw and pass the ball between each other, giggling and laughing the entire afternoon. They had never met before and quickly formed a bond. Eventually, they abandoned the ball and went to the stream where Henrietta L'utile taught them to skip rocks on the water, just like her father had shown her earlier that morning.

While shaking the pea gravel dust from her skirt and backing away from the stream's edge, Henrietta Pompeux asked, brow tightly knit together, "Well how will we ever know to whom we're speaking? We all have the same name."

"I know! Let's all go by our last names!" Henrietta Abram blurted out.

"That sounds a little too formal to me," said Henrietta L'utile, trying to skip a stone across the stream.

"All right..." said Henrietta Pompeux, arms crossed, brow still creased. "What about we use the first letter of our last name?"

"Oh, and let's use our short names! I'll be Henny A!" giggled Henrietta Abram.

"And I'm Henny L," smiled Henrietta L'utile.

"And I'm Henny P!" proclaimed Henrietta Pompeux with the definiteness of her father.

The three were inseparable the entire summer, meeting in the park every morning and waiting until Henny P's nanny went to knit. Soon, they would play, and laugh, and roam around their little neighborhood area, always ending up at the stream for stone skipping. Eventually, their tête-à-tête-à-tête progressed into venturing to the pâtisserie after stone skipping. The man at the pâtisserie already knew of the three girls who shared the birthday, as it was his wife who delivered Henny L. Every morning, he would give each girl a roll or a Danish when they came to say "Hello," and they would sit in front of the shop, playing like they were sophisticated ladies until the baker would tell them they had been away from the park too long.

They held nothing back from each other, and soon had no secrets, knowing each other's wishes, likes, and dreams. When one started a sentence, another would finish it. When one girl forgot her hat, the other two would take theirs off.

They knew Henny L wanted to work with animals, while Henny A loved flowers, and Henny P... well, she wanted to become a famous artist and have a painting hung in the Hôtel de Ville art show.

One day, two years after their meeting, the three were walking arm in arm in arm to the pâtisserie. They were stopped by some official looking men, all in gray, with serious faces and guns over their shoulders. *"Achtung! Wohin geht ihr drei?"*

All three just looked up with seven-year-old silence and big round eyes.

"Ich frage euch schon wohin ihr drei ghet?" barked the man in gray with the gun.

All three let out a shriek and ran for the park. Once there, they decided they should all go to their own homes and not say a word about the scary men at the pâtisserie.

Henny P's father was happy and dancing around the room with her mother when she came in the door. "What's... what's going on?" she asked, taking off her hat and hanging it on the peg by the door.

"Today is a special day! A special and blessed day indeed!" laughed and smiled her father, leaving Henny P's mother and taking her up in his arms. She'd never seen him so giddy and began to smile and laugh with him as he danced around the room. "Today, my dear daughter, we become even more respected and powerful than before!"

"But papa, aren't we already respected?"

"Oh no! Not like this! No! We'll be among the premiere families in the country." Henri put his daughter down and knelt before her. "You see my dear, today I received my commission. I am a colonel in the Reich's Army!"

Henny A quietly opened her front door and noticed all the shades were drawn, no one in the front room. She heard muffled voices in the basement and went to the kitchen door leading down.

"I tell you; I will not leave!" she heard her father shout. "Why should we abandon all we built here, huh? I ask you. Why is it I should leave? I've done nothing wrong."

"But Isaac, we have six young girls, their lives will be…"

"No! I will not even think about leaving what is mine. It. Is. Mine! This house, this village, this place... They. Are. Mine! That is the end of it. I will fight, I will hide. I will quietly attack. But I will never leave. That is all I should say."

Henny L walked through the front door and there stood her father, looking at a picture of Henny L's mother on the ancient fireplace mantle.

"Hello, Papa."

"There's my little Hen," he smiled down on her.

She returned a grin and looked up into his sad eyes. "What's wrong, Papa?"

"Oh, my baby girl, our town is going to have some trouble soon."

"Papa, is it because of the gray men? Are they making you sad?"

Etienne frowned, giving her his full attention, kneeling next to her. "Where did you see men in gray?"

She saw his eyes were very serious and didn't want to tell him, but somehow knew he needed to know. "We were on our way to the pâtisserie, and the men in gray started yelling at us in a language we don't know."

Etienne put his hands gently on her shoulders. "Who were you with?"

"Just my friends, Henny A and Henny P." Henny L looked down at her feet and felt in some way she'd broken a sacred trust with her sisters.

"Are Henny A and Henny P friends of yours from school?" asked her Papa, still with concern in his voice.

"Oh, no! I've known them longer than that! They're the girls from the park, they're my name sisters! Henny A is Henrietta Abram, she lives on the other side of the park, behind the church with the pretty six-pointed star on top. And Henny P is Henrietta Pompeux, she lives…" Henny L stopped and furrowed her brow. "I know she lives on the other side of the park from us and Henny A but, I'm not sure what house."

Etienne still had a concerned look on his face but reached up and ran his fingers through his daughter's hair. "My dear, things are about to change around our little village. We're not going to be able to go out and about and play with our

friends when we want to for a while." He cupped her face
with his right hand. "Do you understand?"

Henny L shook her head gently, looking up at him with
big eyes that had tears dangling in the trough at the bottom.
"Papa, did I do something wrong?"

Etienne took a deep breath and let it out. "No, my dear,
dear girl. You did nothing wrong. The men in gray are from
over the great river to the east, called the Rhine. They are in
charge of the village now, so they have new rules we'll have
to follow."

"Like when we play a new game?"

Etienne's lips gave a slight smile, but his eyes were tinged
with sadness. "Yes, like when we play a new game. But this
game is more dangerous. So, you will have to ask me before
you go out to the park for a while. We need to learn the rules
before we know how to play. All right? Can you help me
around the house for a while?"

Henny L knew she would miss the other French Hens,
but she nodded and said, "Yes, Papa."

"Good girl." He stood, "Now, remember the secret
rooms in the basement and attic? Why don't you help me get
them cleaned up. I have a feeling we might need them."

"Papa, why do we have secret rooms in the house?" she
asked following him like a little chick behind her mother.

"Because of a war many, many years ago. Your great,
great, great... All right, a lot of greats—grandfather, built
this house during a war. Then, another war came along..."

"What was it called, Papa?"

"Well, we call it the Thirty Years War now. Anyway, your many-greats grandpa and grandma decided to make some hidden rooms, in case they needed to be helpful and hide some friends."

"Did they ever use them?"

"Oh yes, my little Hen, they used them many times." Etienne took a large flour sack full of twine and handed it to Henny L. "Here you are. Take this to the shed out back, then come back for more. I have a feeling we'll be needing to help some friends sooner than later."

One month went by. Then two, and three, and six. One very late evening there was a quiet but insistent rapping on the back door of the leaning house across the stream. Etienne went to the door and looked out the kitchen window to see who was without. He had never seen the woman covered with a blanket before, but he had seen the little girl.

He opened the door and asked, "May I help you?"

At the door was a woman wearing only one shoe and a blanket—nothing else. She was dirty and bruised and had a deep cut over her left eye where someone had obviously hit her. Standing next to her was a little barefoot girl wearing only a night shirt.

"I'm… I'm Golda Abram. Your daughter Henrietta and my daughter are friends."

Golda burst into tears and crumpled to the ground. "We have nothing. They… they… they…"

Etienne looked in both directions outside the door, and said, "Hurry, come in," helping them to the kitchen table, then locking and bolting the door.

"Papa…" came the sleepy voice of Henny L from behind him.

"Come, my little Hen," he said over his shoulder while sitting directly in front of Golda.

"Henny A!" squealed Henny L with delight. Her smile quickly turned to a confused frown when she saw the state she was in.

"Hen, why don't you take your friend up to your bed-room. I think they'll be staying with us for a while."

"Really?" asked Henny L, suddenly wide awake. She went to Henny A and gave her a big hug. "Come on Henny A, let's go upstairs, I'll show you my room."

After crawling into bed, Henny L snuggled into Henny A, who was stiff, cold, and staring straight ahead. She asked, "You, okay?"

No reply came. Henny A continued looking forward, not blinking. After a long silent time, she said without emotion, "My Papa and five sisters, they're all gone. Three gray men came to our house. I was already in bed, but snuck part way down the stairs." She again became silent for a long time. "They shot my Papa when he told them to leave. Then, they took three of my sisters outside and I heard gun shots. One of the gray men took my oldest sister outside. I heard her cry and scream. She kept yelling, 'No, no, no… don't do… Please don't…' and after about ten minutes she stopped crying, she stopped screaming. It was quiet."

Henny A spoke with no emotion. Her fingers were curling into fists, then opened again. "The older gray man with the long black boots grabbed mamma and tore off her dress. He started hitting and punching her with his fists. He undid his pants."

"Why'd he undo his pants?" asked Henny L.

Henny A slowly shook her head, looking forward with wide eyes, like she was still seeing what was happening on the white wall across from her.

"How'd you get away?"

"When the gray man was laying on top of Mamma, she saw me on the stairs and bit the gray man's ear off. When the gray man reached up to where his ear used to be, Mamma grabbed my hand, and we ran here."

Henny L gently wrapped her arms around her friend and said, "Try to go to sleep. My Papa will know what to do in the morning." They lay like that for a long time. Not moving, barely breathing. Then, as if an ice cube were melting, a soft warm, wet drop landed onto Henny L's shoulder, then another, and Henny A convulsed in an unstoppable flow of tears.

The war raged on and on around the three French Hens for many years. Sometimes it was close, other times it was across the great river Rhine to the east. The three didn't know anything about politics or religion or hatred; all they knew is they liked and trusted each other. They swore silence, that no one would know about Henny A and her mother, living with Henny L and her father; or the two other people living in the secret rooms in the attic and basement. They were birth/name sisters. That's all they needed to know. Whenever there was a lull, and when Papa Etienne or Mamma Abrams said it was all right, the three would sneak away, getting together on the bank of the stream running in front of Henny L's house, laughing and playing and chasing, as if there were no problems in the world…and yes, skipping stones across the water. They'd heard terms like Kike, and Hebe, and Nazi, and Kraut. But they were only words. *Nothing* could keep them apart.

One awful night, shelling breached the ridge to the West. There were men in green, running and shooting anything moving. Buildings burst apart and flames engulfed their exposed remains.

Much as the night many years before, there came a hurried knocking at kitchen door. This time Henny L was first to arrive. She looked out the window and saw Henny P, clothes torn and charred, barefoot. Henny L threw open the door and caught her as she fainted away.

Two days later Henny P woke in a bed with clean sheets, a pitcher of fresh flowers on the bedside table, and two smiling Henny faces looking down on her.

"We thought you'd sleep forever!" cackled Henny A.

"What day is it?" asked Henny P, trying to prop herself up on her elbows.

"You've been asleep for two days," said Henny L quietly, putting a fresh cold compress on Henny P's forehead.

Henny P lay back in the bed and stared forward. "They're gone. It's all… gone."

"Who's gone, what's gone?" asked Henny A.

"My house, my mother, my…" She closed her eyes tight. "My father." A single tear left her right eye. "The house was hit by a shell and my mother was trapped and burning under a beam when I crawled out. My father ran from the house, pistol drawn while trying to put on his uniform jacket, but…" she looked up at the two for the first time, "he was shot down by the troops coming in."

The girls sat together in silence until Henny P said, "And now, I'm alone. I have no one."

"No. Not true," said Henny A.

"You've got us. You'll always have us," smiled Henny L with tears rolling down her cheeks.

The brutality of war finally ended, and the Hens moved on. All three and moved from the only village they'd ever known and loved. They married, had children, and grandchildren. Etienne and Golda both passed in time, as did all three Hen's husbands; and fifty years went as if in a blink of an eye.

Henny L was the first to return to the village after her Jordan passed. He was the son of the baker at the pâtisserie the Henny's frequented when they were young. He and Henny L had opened their own pâtisserie three towns away and she had a house full of children, dogs, and cats. But Saverne was still home, and she had always dreamt of coming back to the place she and her Papa had loved so well.

Henny A's love of flowers not only gained her a position rebuilding parks all over France after the war, but introduced her to the love her life, Emil. Emil was an immigrant from the remnants of Dresden after it was leveled in the war. Before the war, he was a botanist at the University. After he was freed from the Terezin Camp, he came to France to get a new start. The two enjoyed thirty-three wonderful years together. But eventually Emil's health gave way and Henny A was left all alone. Her children had all moved to other countries and started new lives. She moved back to where it all started, Saverne; and into the old leaning house by the stream with Henny L.

Henny P moved to Paris and followed her artistic dream. She never did have a showing in the Hôtel de Ville of Saverne, no. However, she did show at the Louvre, the Academia in Florence, and the Prado in Madrid. After studying in Chicago, she married the gallery owner of Williams in

New York, a Mr. Billy Williams. She painted, she taught, she raised two beautiful children who moved across America to the far coast. The children asked her to move in with them after Billy Williams passed, but she realized she missed the slow, relaxed pace of life in Saverne and decided to move back.

The day after her arrival, she walked back past her old house on the far side of the park. It had been beautifully restored. She wondered who the new owners were and almost knocked. She couldn't erase the last visions of the devastation from her mind, so she walked away with a small tear creeping down her left cheek, and around the corner to where the old pâtisserie used to be.

Her heart skipped three beats as she saw it. Nothing about it had changed, except there were more tables out front on the street. As she approached, she saw two unmistakable faces. There sitting at their "usual table" were Henny A and Henny L.

Without a word, Henny P joined them and sat in her seat, the same she sat in when she was five years old. Henny A and Henny P were speechless. The three stared at each other silently. Henny L put up her hand to dry the tears trail on Henny P's cheek, and Henny P reached out for Henny A's hand. No words were exchanged, only smiles, tears, and hugs for the next fifteen minutes. The Hens had come back to roost.

All three live in the old leaning house by the stream across from the city park. They take care of each other, cook for each other, and are there for each other when nightmares wake them in the night.

But, what everyone in town silently looks toward is Tuesday evenings. Every Tuesday evening, come rain or shine, just after dinner, you'll see the three Hens, sitting in chairs at the edge of the stream, taking turns… skipping stones across the old stream.

FOUR CALLING BIRDS

Four Calling Birds

Jerry was a colicky baby. Exasperated, his mother would give up. She would dress him in his baby giraffe and seals jumper, strap him in his pram, and walk him around the neighborhood until he'd drop off. At some point in the middle of the night he would wake, but instead of crying out, he'd smile at a small yellow bird on the foot rail of his crib. The bird would bob and flap its wings and open its beak, but no sound would come out. He would stare at the bird and its gyrations until he fell back into a deep and dream-filled sleep.

Linda was a very sweet child; quiet, respectful, alert. She would sit for hours listening to stories told by the stray men her mother would bring home, only to be sent to bed, often without supper, and fall asleep, trying to block out the laughing and giggling emanating from the other room. She'd float in a dreamless sleep, eventually waking to a little blue bird sitting on the footboard of her bed, flapping its wings and dancing around, chirping soundlessly. She would begin to smile and quietly giggle, drifting off to vibrant dreams until the sun's first rays woke her.

Louis was a fun-loving little boy but was always in the wrong place at the wrong time. He remembered being in the back seat of the car when a big truck came. After the truck, he remembered a big wooden box and how sad everyone was, telling him his mother was inside. He remembered his father, sitting with a glass of tea in a short glass and holding a picture of his mother, crying as he poured more tea in the glass from a bottle with a cork on top. Louis would go to bed, pulling the covers over his head when he heard his father stagger into the bathroom, yelling, "Who the hell put the lid down on the toilet?" He'd clamp his eyes shut and fall asleep in a tight ball. When he'd startle awake, there'd be a bright green bird flapping its wings, bobbing up, down, and from side to side on the windowsill. The bird opened its beak and swung it from side to side like a silent trombone. He didn't remember going back to sleep but would hear his father's alarm going off in a distant bedroom, waking him from a peace-filled dream.

Anita loved to laugh but didn't get many opportunities. Both of her lips didn't go from side to side like other kids. No, the top lip stopped just under her nose, showing her top teeth. Her grandmother took her to preschool at the "Open Arms of Love Pentecostal Church," but after the first cartoon and snack, her grandmother picked her up. The staff thought her lip was "too distracting." At night she played, all alone, with her baby doll or pony till bedtime. The only time her grandmother had time for her was to tuck the covers under her chin, saying, "Now don't be no trouble tonight. The angels don't take kindly to no trouble makin' kids." A sharp knocking sound would wake Anita in the middle of the night, and she'd see something move on the dresser. A little red bird would bounce and flap its wings clapping its beak open and closed, but never make any sound. She'd smile a crooked smile and drift off to dream sweet dreams.

An entire lifetime went by, and the four children grew and grew, forgetting all about the four call-less birds. They each had partners and children or were married to their jobs. Some traveled to far-flung exotic lands, other stayed in place and kept the home fires burning. Some had children and grandchildren, others just enjoyed the giggles, tears, and tantrums of the young from afar. As the four became older, they began to slow. Their sight became a bit dimmer, and they had to turn the sound up a little louder. They lost spouses and partners, eventually finding they couldn't be or shouldn't be alone anymore.

By an odd twist of fate, the four—Jerry, Linda, Louis, and Anita—moved to "Serenity's Song Adult Care Facility" on the same day. After settling in that first day, each, in their own way, realized this was their last stop. They silently asked themselves deep and different questions. "Did my life make a difference?" Or "Does it matter I never went to Madagascar, or climbed Kilimanjaro? Or "Why didn't I write a best seller?"

The four gathered in the commons room for their orientation, feeling like it was the first day of school.

"Hey, I'm Jerry. What's your name?" he asked with bright eyes, wearing a Pioneer Corn seed cap and plaid shirt while shuffling to the table.

"Hello Jerry. I'm Linda. I just arrived today." She stopped herself short. "Well, that was a rather obvious statement wasn't it, since this *is* the orientation meeting."

Jerry sat and they smiled at each other as another woman using a walker passed, sitting with a rough 'plop' in the chair next to Linda.

"Hello there! And who might you be?" asked Jerry with a big white smile.

When she spoke, she raised her hand to cover her scarred mouth. "I'm Anita."

"Sorry? You say your name's Mita?" asked Jerry, tapping his ear. "It's 'bout time for a new battery."

"No, Anita." She lowered her hand so he could read her lips.

"Oh! Anita!" Jerry's upper plate slipped, coming halfway out of his mouth as he said her name. He caught the teeth a moment before they clattered across the table and held them up like a trophy, laughing, "Little buggers almost got away from me," then slipped them back into his mouth with no sign of embarrassment.

Anita smiled behind her hand and ever so slowly brought it down to the table. She relaxed at Jerry's lack of shame and boisterous nature.

Another gentleman, dressed quite well, glided to the table with the grace and ease of a dancer. He sat, but looked forward, not focusing on anything. His cheeks were rosy and his hair perfectly coiffed, but there was no life in his eyes.

"Are you alright?" asked Linda with concern.

"Me? Oh, oh yes. I just. Well, I lost my..." He closed his eyes tightly. "I'm fine. Just a bit... maudlin, that's all." He glanced up with a sad smile, looking like an old basset hound.

"Oh, you poor dear," said Linda. "Losing someone close is the worst feeling in the world." She took one of his smooth hands in her gnarled fist.

He looked up at her, "Yes. Yes, it is."

The four bonded at this first meeting, becoming inseparable. Eating every meal together, telling stories and jokes, playing games they hadn't thought of in forty, sixty, seventy years. They came to know each other's hearts and minds, and as intimately as their children, spouses, or partners. Maybe better.

One warm December night Louis could have sworn he saw something move on his windowsill as he drifted off to sleep. When he woke around 3 a.m., he felt something familiar in the room. He turned to the sill and saw a small green bird, flapping its wings, bobbing up and down. Its beak opened and closed like it was soundlessly singing. He didn't question why it was there. It simply *felt* like it belonged, like he had always known the little creature.

In the morning he relayed what he thought was a dream to his friends, only to find they *all* had been visited by birds, each a different color: red, blue, and yellow; but all bobbing and flapping, singing a soundless song.

After a full minute of awkward silence, Jerry said, "Well, I'm not going to let it change what I do. It's a little strange, I mean... dancing birds and soundless chirping." He shrugged and said, "But hey! Life is strange." He then fell into a short burst of laughter ending in a slight cough.

"I've worked with birds." started Anita, brow furrowed. "I've never seen that kind of behavior exhibited with humans."

"I've been called 'bird brain' a few times but... I never thought it might be true!" joked Louis.

"Yeah, I've got 'bird legs' but I didn't know I was *one of the family*!" laughed Linda.

The four giggled raucously enough to catch the attention of a caretakers, who came over to see if everything was all right. That evening all four were curious if the birds would reappear. Jerry awoke after a dream that quickly faded into the recesses of his mind. He thought he remembered being with his wife but... it just slipped away. He turned over and, there was his little yellow bird on the sill.

"So? What are you doing here?"

A silent 'chirp' left the bird's beak as it cocked its head... first left, then right and, bobbed twice.

"Huh... So, do you have a voice or has the cat got your tongue? Well, do you have a message or are you just here to amuse?"

Again, it chirped silently, and Jerry slipped into slumber, his mind hearing a very small, light, but clear voice asked him, *"What is your favorite memory of life? What will you remember forever?"*

Jerry's dreams drifted back to his wedding day, the birth of his daughter and son. He saw his seventh-year birthday present, a sled he'd ride down the back hill every winter. He saw his wife's face when she said 'yes' to his awkward proposal. His dreams never moved to work, or money, or power. What made him *happy* was his relationships, the *friendships* he'd built with the people he loved.

When he came down for breakfast, Linda was already at the table with oatmeal and half a grapefruit before her. Jerry walked up and she shot him a sly smile.

"You saw it again, didn't you?"

He quietly walked to her right, sitting with a broad smile. "Yes, I did. And you know what else?"

"What?"

"I spoke to it."

"You what?"

"I spoke to it." He unwrapped his cutlery and spread it out.

"So? What'd it say?" Linda asked, eyes wide.

Jerry took a bite of his toast and chewed, smile still on his face. "Nothing. Well not really."

"What do you mean not really?"

Jerry put his toast down. "I asked why it was here and if it had a message."

"And? What did it say?"

"*Nada.* Little bugger did its silent chirp thing and I fell back to sleep. But..." he pointed a finger at the ceiling. "I thought I heard a question." He pointed to his head. "In here."

"Well? What did it ask?"

Jerry sat back in his chair. "What my favorite memories were. What I'd remember forever." He stared ahead for a long ten seconds before picking up his spoon.

Linda let out a slight gasp, bringing her hand to her mouth. "No..."

"Yes," answered Jerry, dipping his spoon into his oatmeal.

"No. I mean yes... but no." She stared ahead as if she'd seen a ghost.

"Okay. I'll bite. Yes, means no, and no means, yes?"

"No! I mean I..." She looked around the room then lowered her voice, leaning into Jerry, eyes wide. "Jerry, I dreamt of all my favorite things last night. I mean *all* of them!"

"Come on! You're just saying that." He looked at her with disbelieving eyes.

"No Jerry! I mean it!" She leaned back and lowered her voice again, taking his hand. "I dreamt of all the things that meant anything to me. My first dog, my first husband's first Christmas gift to me, the first time I saw the pyramids, the…" She smiled and looked down at the table, then retrieved a crumpled tissue from her sweater pocket and dabbed a tear forming in her right eye.

"So, what happened?"

"Alright you two, get a room," said Louis as he and Anita came walking toward the pair. Jerry released Linda's hand and sat back.

"OK, you caught us! We might as well tell 'em Linda. We're eloping next week to 'Happy Acres' down the road."

"Great! We'll tie strings of empty Ensure cans to the back of your golf cart."

All four laughed as Louis and Anita sat, trays and coffee in tow.

"So, I'm curious," asked Jerry looking first at Louis then Anita. "Did you two dream last night?"

They both looked at each other and then silently at the tabletop. "I don't think I dreamt about anything last night," said Louis still looking down at the table.

"Bessie," said Anita, almost whispering.

"Excuse me?" asked Linda.

"Bessie and Dot," smiled Anita. "They were two dear, dear friends when I was a very young child. Bessie was a little girl in my neighborhood that I would play with when my grandma would let me. She was blind from birth and didn't..." She took a deep breath. "... She didn't make fun of my lip."

"Who was Dot?" asked Jerry.

"Dot was the neighbor's dog." Anita had a broad grin from ear to ear, not trying to hide her scar. She looked up at Linda. "She's the reason I became a Vet." Anita looked back down at the table, trying to keep the memory with her as long as possible.

Louis looked at the table, obviously trying to avoid eye contact. "So why the question about our dreams?"

"Jerry had a little chat with his bird last night," said Linda, putting her tissue back in her pocket.

Both Anita and Louis looked at Jerry with wide eyes. He looked back at them with the look a six-year-old gives when he knows the answer to a secret before anyone else knows there's a question.

"Well?"

Jerry retold the tale to Louis and Anita, and the table fell silent again.

That night, all four tried to stay awake, but still fell asleep. Linda stirred around four a.m. and looked out her window, noticing something flit between her and the full moon. There, in silence, sat a blue bird bobbing and weaving as it had done the previous night.

"How are you, little bird? What are you doing here, or is it a secret that you can't tell me?"

It sat chirping silently, wings out and flapping.

She watched it, amused, and felt herself drifting back to sleep, hearing in a small, high, clear voice, *"Who were your friends? Who was friendly to you when no one else dared?"*

Immediately a flood of memories churned in her soul. Friends—in school days, in work, in travel. She remembered a little girl she had taken under her wing. Rose, who had lost her mother and father to an accident one March evening. Then a different scared little girl of ten, Geri, popped into her memories. Geri's mother left one day for work in April, never to return. She adopted both girls the following year.

In the morning, Linda came to the table where Jerry already sat.

"Well?"

"Well, what?" asked Jerry.

"You know perfectly well, 'Well what?' Don't be coy. It's not becoming in a man your age."

Jerry laughed a deep belly laugh. "Touché!"

"Well?" Linda asked again.

"I figured I'd wait until the other two showed up before I spilled.

"You don't have long to wait," said Anita, coming to the table from behind them with Louis trailing her.

"It's about time!" shot Linda with fake ire.

"Oh, oh, oh... I think someone's been dreaming again." said Louis with a grand smile.

"Well, yes. Yes, I *have*, if you must know," said Linda with a slight edge.

"Oh, calm yourself my dear," said Louis patting her hand. "Anita and I have already compared notes. It seems, we are in agreement. We're all going collectively mad."

"But did you have any visitors?" asked Linda.

All three looked at her, then at each other.

"My dear, how did you know that?"

"Simple, Louis," she smiled, "a little birdie told me."

All eyes stayed glued to her as she sipped at her coffee silently.

"Oh, for Pete's sake!" blurted out Anita, which made all four of them let out a nervous laugh.

"All right, all right..." started Linda. "It came to me at around four..."

"Mine at two."

"Mine at three-thirty"

"Mine at four."

After Linda told her dream experience, Louis took a deep breath and stared at a single spot in the middle of the table. "I saw... I saw my mother." As soon as he said her name, "Marge," tears flowed past his smiling dimples onto the faux wood tabletop. "I haven't seen my mother since she died in a car accident when I was very young. She looked exactly the same. She didn't say anything. No. She just came to me and held me, just like she used to. While…" Louis cleared his throat, trying to collect himself enough to continue, "While she held me, she hummed *All the Pretty Little Horses* to me, like she used to do every night when she put me to bed." He continued to stare at the spot as Anita began to hum the tune. By the second line Linda sang the line, "…Go to sleep little baby." She was joined by the rest of the table, "You shall have, all the pretty little horses…"

As the tune faded, Jerry said in a 'matter of fact' tone, "Well you know what this means."

"No, what?" asked Anita, her coffee cup strategically lingering in front of her lips.

"This means that we're either all delusional or…" He took a deep breath and let it out slowly. "We're all being visited by aliens."

The other three all protested at the same time.

"Aw, this is ridiculous!" Jerry pushed himself up to his feet. "I think somebody's slipping us a Mickey before bed and we're dreaming what they want us to dream." He picked up his tray and walked toward the dish return, saying over his shoulder, "Besides, it's almost time for last night's Jeopardy rerun; whose ass am I gonna kick?"

That night all four went to bed at their normal times. Weeks went by and the four had intermittent visits and dreams from the four birds. Then on Christmas Eve, many families visited the facility. Jerry's daughter and grandchildren came for a part of the day, and Linda's grand-niece came to visit with her two-year-old daughter. Anita heard laughing and giggling as she turned the corner into Linda's room and froze at the sight of the two-year-old girl on Linda's lap. She was beautiful, but her upper lip had a split in the middle all the way up to her nose. Flashes of emotions, and name-calling, and lack of friends whirled in her mind.

"Anita, I want you to meet my daughter and grand-daughter. Emily, this is my best friend, Anita." Linda turned to the girl on her lap. "And this little one is Julia." Julia looked up at Anita with big blue eyes. The corners of Anita's lips tipped up and a single tear formed in her left eye as Julia reached up and touched the scar on her upper lip, just below her nose. Linda started to reach for the child's hand but stopped when she saw Anita kiss Julia's little hand, then reach out to hug her close.

The Christmas Eve events began to slow down after the community's sing-along and gift exchange. Before all turned in, the four met back at Jerry's room for their holiday tradition, a nightcap from a smuggled-in bottle of Maker's Mark brought by his goddaughter. Jerry raised his paper cup and cleared his throat. "To what we've seen, are seeing now, and will see. To whatever our futures hold, may they always be what we want, and not what we deserve."

They all drank their cups down.

Jerry's eyes became a bit misty. "I want you all to know I, uh... I love you very much. I mean, I've never been too open with my feelings but. I just… Well, I just thought you'd each like to know that I've never had better, closer, or more meaningful friends." He poured a little more in his cup and drank deeply, then wiped his nose with a handkerchief he pulled out of his back pocket.

The other three stood for a moment in complete silence. They had been taken by surprise with Jerry's candor. He'd always been the jokester, the prankster, the grounded one.

"Jerry, what's up?" asked Linda, somewhat suspect.

"Up? Nothing's up. I just, well, I thought it was about time I told my best friends how much they meant to me. Nothing has to be up. Now," he forced a smile as a tear dropped from his eye. "Get out! I need my beauty sleep."

Before the three went to their respective rooms to await the morning, Louis went to Jerry and offered his hand, looking him deeply in his eyes. They both had tears forming but smiled through them as he grasped Louis's hand, shaking it.

Sometime in the middle of the night Anita was awakened to the sweetest voice she'd ever heard. It was high and light and melodic. She opened her eyes to her little red bird. "I, I can hear you!" she said with a start. The little bird stopped singing and looked at her.

"Yes, Anita, you can hear me."

"But how is that possible? And how is it I can understand what you're saying?"

"Anita, all will become clear to you soon, if you choose."

"I don't understand."

"Anita, I am not just a bird," the figure hopped to the edge of the windowsill and fluttered down toward the floor, changing in mid-air, the red fading into a pink, then a dazzling white. The head morphed into a beautiful face with flowing black hair; the only constant was the pair of dark, kind eyes. "Anita, I'm your guardian angel. I've been with you your entire life."

"I, I don't remember seeing you before."

"I don't actually look like this. What you see now is how your mind sees me as an angel. I've always been here. When you were born, I used to sing to you and help you drift off to sleep."

"I don't remember."

"You wouldn't. As you grew older, you couldn't hear me any longer, but you saw me dance and bob silently. You lost your sense of hearing and seeing God's voice and his creature—me— with your ears and eyes and began to with your heart."

"So, why am I hearing you now?"

"Because it's time for you to make a major choice. You need to decide if you want to go home or stay and help a friend in need."

"Home? You mean…"

"Yes, Anita. I can take you now, if you like."

"Or…" she began to slowly shake her head. "Or I can stay and help a friend? Who? What can I do?"

"You have seen Linda's grandniece's daughter, Julia. Yes?"

"Yes." Anita looked away, avoiding her guardian's gaze.

"You know the challenges Julia will face. She, and Emily could both learn from you, with love and generosity."

"I..." she turned toward her angel with tears in her eyes. "I don't understand, why did God make her like that?" she swallowed and looked back up at her guardian. "Why did God make..." she broke down, overcome with emotion.

"Why did God make you the way he did? Is that what you want to know?"

Anita nodded her head slowly, not looking up.

The angel seemingly sat on the edge of the bed, facing her. "No one knows why God gives challenges in life, why one person has one advantage, and another has three disadvantages. I do know that what you are, is not what you see or feel here." The angel raised his hand to her head. "Yes, you are in this body for a time, but it will all too soon go away. No. What you are is the spirit *within* this shell. That is the real you." The angel stood back up. "No human knows God's mind. Nor do any of the angels, for that matter. My guess is, God gave you a special blessing with your physical infirmity. You have been a blessing to so many; animals *and* like souled people in your life. That is a true gift that few humans have, and *that* is a gift, born from this so-called infirmity."

Anita again silently nodded her head, looking down.

"Now, I must ask you for your answer. Will I be taking you home, or will you stay to help and guide Julia?"

The next morning Anita came into the dining room after having one of the deepest and best sleeps in her many years. Linda was already sitting at the table and had been crying.

"They're gone," said Linda, wiping her nose with a tissue.

"Who?"

"Louis and Jerry, they're gone."

"But they..." Anita stopped herself. It made sense. Jerry and Louis had been talking more and more about what their birds had been saying to them a couple nights before. And, she'd had the same question posed to her mere hours ago. It made sense that Jerry and Louis had gone home. Jerry missed his wife, and Louis missed his partner.

Anita sat and quietly put her arm around Linda's back. "Did your bird come last night?"

Linda silently looked at Anita out of the corner of her eye.

"It's not a bird, you know," Anita said under her breath. "They *knew* they were going,"

"They what?"

"They knew they were going."

Linda looked at Anita, then nodded slowly, "How do *you* know?" then she leaned in.

"I was given the same choice last night, to stay or go." she looked back at Linda. "And you?"

Linda looked down at the table, then back at Anita. "I chose to stay to help my great-niece and her daughter for a time." She wiped her eye and looked at Anita. "Why'd you choose to stay?"

"To help a friend with her daughter and great-niece." Anita reached out and took Linda's hand as strains of *"What Child is this…"* were heard on a TV down the hall.

Over the years Anita helped Linda with her great-niece. Julia was a bright, joy-filled child with a spirit to match her inner beauty. A year after they'd met, Julie had the first surgery to straighten her lip; and over the next two years, she made wonderful progress. Soon, she was smiling like most other children. But there were some other scars that just didn't heal easily. These were the scars with which Anita helped.

Then, one evening, years later, before she went to bed, Anita stopped by Linda's room.

"Knock, knock."

"Come in *please!*"

"I just wanted to thank you for letting me go with you to Julia's seventh grade recital. The party after was marvelous."

"Oh please! It wouldn't have been a celebration without you. You know that."

"Well, I sometimes think that I take your family for granted and I think…" She looked down and away, "…that they're my very own. I just wanted to thank you for letting me be the 'tag-along' sometimes."

"Anita, really! Don't you *ever* think that way. Never, ever again! You're as much family as I am. In fact, she looks more to you for advice than me."

"Well, all I know is, that girl is special. She's one in a million and I'm glad I've gotten to know her." Anita looked away. "And I love her like she's my own."

They both sat in silence for a few minutes before Linda looked up at Anita. "I've, um… I've got to talk to you about something," said Linda, suddenly looking away

"What's that?"

"I've… I've been getting a visitor every night this week.

"Oh? Anyone I know?"

Linda smiled and took Anita's hands in hers.

Anita sat silently for a minute and then smiled back. "I'm gonna miss you. Ya know?"

Linda kept smiling, shaking her head as a tear dropped. "I'm going to miss you, too."

Anita stood and went to Linda, wrapping her arms around her in a tender embrace that only best friends understand with tears of mixed emotions running down their cheeks.

"All right now. Go on to bed."

Anita got to the door before Linda's voice stopped her. "Do me a favor?"

Anita didn't look back but stood, looking into the hallway. "What?"

"Watch over our family for me."

Anita turned to look at her, knowing it'd be the last time she'd see her in this world. "I will." She mentally took a picture of her best friend. "I love you."

Linda smiled back. "I love you, too."

Anita turned and shuffled down the hall to her own room, tears flowing freely. At four in the morning, she woke to her little red bird bobbing and singing its song in the windowsill. As she watched, it was joined by a little blue bird. The duet was beautiful, unworldly so. A few minutes later they were joined by a green and a yellow feathered friend. The quartet made Anita smile, weep, and giggle, as memories of her friends danced and chuckled in her mind. The song they sang was the most heartfelt praise of nature she'd ever heard.

As the song faded and the birds flew and danced in the air, ever upward, Anita knew her three best friends would visit one more time—maybe soon, maybe a few years away. But it would be when the time was right, she would hear the song of the four calling birds—join them and fly away—ever singing as they flew.

FIVE GOLDEN RINGS

Five Golden Rings

"Aw Honey... just one more cup?"

The mousey blonde dipped her chin and looked across the counter into the red and soupy eyes of an elderly man. He wore a four-day, five o'clock shadow, and clothes too tattered for a thrift store. After glancing to her left and right she reached for the glass pot, stained brown with coffee. "Alright Joe. But this *has* to be your last one," she whispered, as her stern look melted into a smile.

"Okay, Lucy. It'll be the last one. Promise!" When the man smiled, she saw his eyes sparkle with the road map of wrinkles tightening around them. "Thank you much Lucy. You're very..." he stopped and seemed to be thinking of the right word. "Courteous, ya know that?"

Lucy smiled back at him, "Well... thank you kind sir," and scooted the small stainless pitcher of milk across the old and yellowed, gold-speckled Formica countertop, looking toward the door where Florence, the resident diner matriarch, sat at the register. Lucy had been working at the 'Five Golden Rings' diner—a North Chicago institution—for eight years, and Florence had been perched on the same broken-down stool, torn-up seat pad, every night; unmoving and watching silently as the customers drifted in and out.

"Alright girls, it's time!" Florence demanded in a scratchy, aged, voice. The clock above the door pointed to 2:55 a.m. but the diner staff knew the real time was 2:45. "Last call folks. We need to get outta here!"

"Anything else hon?" asked a high-pitched, slightly too chipper, raven-haired waitress. She bent forward, toward a well-dressed man in his forties, and pulled her biceps together, crossing her arms on the counter in front of her. The effect was not lost on her customer, as his eyes seemed glued to the rather large chasm of flesh in front of him.

He finally looked back up at the black-haired waitress's eyes and blushed, shaking his head no. The man tossed a twenty-dollar bill next to his plate and went to the register to pay.

Lucy walked by her, shaking her head.

The well-endowed waitress looked after Lucy, "What? I need the tips, and they wanna look! What do you want from me?"

"Millie! Music!" Florence yelped from the front of the restaurant.

Millie didn't look up. She was a sunken form seated in the back booth, staring into space more than folding napkins. Millie had a young daughter at home and her husband had left for work a week and and never came home.

"Millie! Music!" came the raspy voice once more.

Millie continued to stare, not hearing the command.

Lucy reached up and flicked off the switch to the stereo before passing through the kitchen's swinging padded red door, the sound of Tommy Dorsey and his band suddenly stopping.

"Thanks!" croaked Florence, not looking up to see who turned the stereo off.

Lucy didn't hear Florence's comment. She was already in the back sorting hot silverware from the dishwasher and slipping it into their correct bins for the girls roll in the napkins in the morning, a.k.a.—in three hours. She came back out and looked for the waitress who closed, Bobbie.

"Florence, have you seen Bobbie?"

"She's gone."

"Gone?"

"Yeah, she said you'd cover her." Florence started to Lucy, not moving, waiting for her response.

Lucy just sighed and dug into the pepper and salt shakers like a woman on a mission. She'd worked a double shift and was in real pain from the miles of walking, and would be right back in here tomorrow morning for the late breakfast rush at ten a.m. She screwed the last cap on the last ketchup bottle, stowed the silverware, then went into the men's room where she found an overflowing trash can. "Just great!" she said under her breath. Ten minutes later the two bathrooms were spruced back up to their semi-pristine 1919 look "The Five Golden Rings" was known for.

Florence sat on her stool with basset hound-like eyes, giving Lucy a silent nod counting out the shift's receipts. "Here ya go, a hundred sixty-three dollars and twenty-three cents for the day." Lucy swept the pile into her open bag and closed the clasp, then put her hand on the door handle and looked back at Florence with a slight smile, "Have a good night." She then walked body, mind, and spirit—all screaming 'tired'—to the "L" station.

At half past nine, and only four hours sleep, Lucy waded right back into the hustle and bustle of the crowded restaurant.

"Miss, tell that *gorilla* in the back, if I'd wanted *scrambled* eggs, I'd have ordered them!"

"I'm sorry sir, what was your order?" asked Lucy pulling out her pad and a pen.

"The *same thing* I *always* order in this dive! *Damn!* Why can't you people get it right?"

Lucy didn't flinch, looking at the man wearing the suit that cost as much as six months' wages. "I'm sorry, sir, but I didn't take your order."

The man looked up at her for the first time. "No. No you didn't. Where's that *cow* who was *pretending* to help me?"

"I'm sorry, sir." Lucy said in an even voice. "Your waitress has stepped away for a moment. I'm sure I can help take care of what you need."

"I doubt it. You don't look like you can handle much."

Lucy kept her cool. "I'm so sorry, sir, if you don't have confidence in me. Let me do this for you, I can ask another waitress to help you. I'm sure they'll be free in ten minutes or so."

"Ten *minutes* or... Oh, *hell* no! I haven't got *that* kind of time! I'm due in court!"

"I'm so sorry, sir. If you'll give me your order, I'll have the cooks do a rush for you."

"Fine," he huffed. "Denver omelet, loose, wheat toast. You know what that means, right?"

"Yes sir. I do," she smiled. "Will there be anything else?"

A short six minutes later, Lucy dropped off his plate. "Here you are sir, one Denver omelet, loose. Just like you ordered," with a smile that could melt butter.

After ten days straight and five double shifts, Lucy flopped face-first onto her bed, still in her clothes, and passed out—asleep. She woke with a start as her cheek met the puddle of drool that had formed on the left side of her mouth. She smacked her lips a couple times and looked at the clock. 3:30 p.m. She'd slept for seven and a half hours, still in her uniform, and not moved once.

She stripped off her pink and white striped dress with big white buttons running up the front and dropped it to the floor. Looking up at her was the logo of the "Five Golden Rings," five onion rings lying on a platter with steam rising, and the date 1919 below, signifying the year the diner opened.

After the uniform dropped to the ground, she looked at her phone and saw a voice message. "Hiya Lucy… Um… I wanted to ask you if, um… Well, I wanted to ask if you'd cover for me tonight. I mean, well my little girl has…"

Lucy was beat, but knew she'd take the extra shift for two reasons. She loved Millie's little girl, and Lucy was trying to save up for business school so she could open her own diner. She really loved doing what she did. The energy, the sense of family, and the idea of giving service to people who really enjoyed good food in a friendly atmosphere. But she was beat and didn't know if she had another double in her.

Four hours later she walked through the diner door. "Evening Florence. How are you?"

Florence looked up at the smiling Lucy and just bounced her head up and down in acknowledgment. "What are you doing here?"

"Oh, Millie's little girl…"

"Excuse me?" came a voice directly behind Lucy at the counter.

Lucy turned around. "Yes?" She smiled at an impeccably dressed older woman.

"Could I trouble you for a coffee please?"

"No trouble at all." Lucy filled the cup before the woman. "Here ya go. Anything else?"

"No, no, honey. Just the coffee for now. Maybe something a little later. Thank you."

"Okay." Lucy turned to go to the kitchen but heard the same voice again.

"Excuse me."

"What can I do for you?"

"Could I trouble you for some sugar and milk?"

"Absolutely." Lucy smiled at the woman as she brought her the items.

"Thank you, dear girl. You see tonight is my wedding anniversary," the woman looked down. "By the way, my name is Judy."

"Well, congratulations Judy! How many years?"

"Oh, it would have been sixty-six."

"Would have been?" Lucy put away her pad and pen and leaned on the counter.

"Yes, deary, my Henry has passed."

"Oh, I'm sorry to hear that."

"Thank you, deary." Judy looked up with a sad smile.

Lucy grinned back at her and reached out for the older woman's hand, "Well, congratulations anyway. It's still a beautiful thing to celebrate."

The woman looked up at Lucy with a worn smile and nodded her head as Lucy went to the register.

"Don't let Judy slow you down," said Florence looking toward the door.

Lucy looked back at Judy sipping her coffee. "She seemed sweet."

"She'll talk your ear off, and your tips will drop."

"Oh, that's all right," assured Lucy, picking up an order. "Today's her anniversary."

Over the course of four hours, the woman stopped Lucy twenty-two times. Lucy heard about Judy's service in WW II and meeting her husband, who had succumbed to cancer. She told how he wasted away but always kept his humor and the sparkle in his eye.

"Henry got out of his sick bed before sunrise to make me heart-shaped pancakes. It was something he did every July 1st, the anniversary of the day we met. He'd bring the pancakes up and say, 'Nuts! I forgot the syrup.'" She smiled with a tear in her eye at the remembrance. "Every year, he'd be back in a few minutes with the syrup and some other gift. But this time, well, he didn't come back." She looked down. "I found him, sitting on the front step, watching the sunrise. He'd passed."

The older woman and her story stayed with Lucy the rest of her shift.

When Lucy counted out her receipts at the end of the night, she watched Florence shift back and forth on the old stool and broken-down pad.

Florence said, "See, told you. I knew your tips would drop," giving zero expression as she stood to fill a couple's coffee in the front booth. When Florence stood, Lucy saw there was no padding left on the stool. It was just a worn cloth shell.

Lucy remembered seeing a pad that looked almost exactly like the one Florence was sitting on at the local bodega at her "L" stop, so the following day, Lucy brought the replacement pad—similar in style and color, with two inches of luxurious foam padding— and snuck it into place when Florence went to the restroom. For ten minutes, Florence hadn't noticed the new padding. As Lucy watched, smiling through the kitchen door, she saw Florence's face scowl as she looked down at the new pad. Florence's eyes shot up around the room as Lucy ducked down behind the kitchen door, a warm feeling of satisfaction spreading through her.

When Lucy came back out onto the floor, she was asked, "Miss, would you help me please?"

She saw two men, one in his twenties, leading an older man who was obviously blind.

"Of course. How can I help you?"

"This is my uncle Chet, and he would like a table in your fine establishment while I take care of some last-minute shopping. I shouldn't be an hour."

"Certainly. Where would you like to sit, sir?"

"I'd love to sit where there's a great view of the Rialto, with little boats going under it, and the gondoliers singing tunes to the people from the back, but as you can see, it'd be wasted on me." The man chuckled, and Lucy joined him.

"How about this, I'll seat you near the waitress station and you can flag one of us down when you need to. We'll even sing an Italian song for you. Does that sound all right?"

Chet chuckled "That sounds fine with me."

Lucy looked for Chet's nephew, but he was gone. "Uh..."

"He's gone, isn't he? My nephew, I mean. He's gone, isn't he?"

Lucy heard the slight hurt in the older man's voice "I'm afraid he is."

"That's all right. He's a busy guy. Too busy to chauffer an old codger like me around."

"Well, let's get you settled in." She gave him her right elbow and guided him to the table.

"Coffee?"

"Sure! And some milk and sweetener, too, if you wouldn't mind. But no sugar. Damn diabetes took my sight."

"No problem."

Lucy checked back on Chet every twenty minutes. Several hours later, after not seeing his nephew, she asked with concern if she could get him anything.

"There *is* something you can do."

"Sure Chet, what is it?"

"Well, it's kind of embarrassing, but I usually find out where the bathroom is when I first walk into a place, but my nephew dropped me off so fast I didn't have the chance to…"

"Oh! No problem. Let me take you." She helped him up and gave him her right elbow.

"Sorry about this but, after twelve cups of coffee, a guy's gotta go!" he laughed.

"I totally understand."

Lucy took him into the restroom, orienting him before leaving. "I'll be just outside the door, so take your time." When she turned toward the front of the diner, her heart sank to the pit of her stomach. She saw the back of Chet's nephew running out the door and jumping into a waiting car that took off with a flurry of flying snow spraying out from behind its tires.

"Oh no…" she said under her breath.

"What's the matter?" asked Chet standing in the doorway of the restroom.

"Chet, I need to ask you something and, well, it's a little personal."

"Shoot."

"It has to do with your nephew. Has he…"

"He left me again, didn't he?" Chet's smile began to fade.

"I don't think he meant to. I think there was a mistake. See, you were in the…"

"He came in, didn't see me, and left. Right?"

Lucy was surprised he had such a good handle on the situation. "Yes. But I think…"

"Nope, he knew I was waiting for him. He's done this to me before."

Lucy looked up at the clock. 11:27. "Is there anyone else I can call for you?"

"Nope."

"Oh."

"Aw, Lucy that's okay. If you just call me a cab, I can get home just fine."

"You sure?"

"Yeah, no problem. If you'd make the call for me?"

"Of course," she smiled. I'll be happy to."

"Uh, oh…" uttered Chet.

"What's wrong?"

"Well, it seems my good-for-nothing nephew lifted my wallet."

Lucy looked out at the weather, then back at Chet standing all alone. "Tell you what, my shift just finished," she retrieved her coat from the hook behind the counter by the door. "The weather is bad, and I was planning on taking a cab home anyway. Wanna share a ride? My treat."

He looked authentically confused. "But I can't pay! What about the coffee?"

"On me." Lucy handed Florence $6.00.

Florence silently shook her head and slipped the money into the drawer.

"Am I tipping you, too?" laughed Chet, with a red face, looking down.

"You *bet* you are. With your wit and presence. So, what'll ya say handsome?" She took his arm. "Ready ta go?"

"All right then," he smiled. "Let's go!"

The next night was December twenty-third, and Florence, without excuse, took the first closing shift off in known history. After Millie and a new waitress were no shows, Lucy was left as the sole closer. She was folding napkins in the back booth when the door's bell jangled, and in came an impeccably dressed man wearing a well-made blue pinstriped double-breasted suit under a camel-colored cashmere over coat. He was older but had deportment.

"How may I help you?"

"I w-would like a piece of p-pie and a c-cup of c-coffee if I might."

"Coming right up. What kind of pie would you like?"

"The c-coconut c-cream please."

"One of my favorites."

Lucy set the silverware and napkin down, then brought the pie and a full coffee cup. "Here ya go. Anything else for you?"

It was past closing time, 2 AM Christmas Eve morning, and the cook turned the music off mid-phrase of Bing singing "*Venite adoremus. Venite...*" Lucy closed her eyes and winced before going back to the kitchen to turn the music back on. She wished the cook a 'Merry Christmas,' and sent him home.

"Sorry about that," she smiled coming back to the man. "He thought everyone was gone."

"Oh! I'm-m s-sorry. Are you c-closed?"

"Technically we are, but please, don't worry about it! Take your time."

"N-no, I should go. But first, may I use your r-re-stroom?"

"Of course! It's at the back by the kitchen door. Please, feel free."

The well-dressed man went past the restroom and through the red kitchen door.

"Sir? The restroom is the *other* door."

He smiled a boyish smile over his shoulder at her and beckoned her with a single finger.

Warily, Lucy went to the kitchen door and peered through to where the man stood. He'd stopped before an ancient and yellowed picture on the wall. In it was a group of twenty-five people in the restaurant from the 1950's, all smiles and standing on a bandstand where the booths now sat. The gentleman pointed at a thin young man on the far right in the photo sitting on the edge of the stage holding the hand of the young lady to his left. It took a few seconds, but Lucy suddenly saw the resemblance.

"Oh, my. That's... you!"

"Mm-hm." The man stood there, arms crossed, looking at the picture with a smile.

"And all these people worked here?"

The man nodded.

Lucy looked at the twenty-five and saw a much younger familiar face. "Is that...?"

He shook his head again. "F-Florence."

"Amazing. I'd heard rumors of Florence being here a while but..." She continued to look and saw a large wooden plaque to the right of the door. "What's that and who are the five older men in suits standing next to it?"

The man came closer to the photo. "That's the original s-s-sign and plaque of the 'Five Golden Rings.' It is very s-special." The man got a faraway look in his eyes. "And those were the five original owners. Before the 'F-Five Golden Rings' opened, the f-five original owners had f-five m-matching golden rings made in honor of their n-new establishment. One n-night after settling on their new menu they w-were j-joking around and named their new diner 'Five Golden Rings'."

"No kidding? I thought it was from the Christmas song, or onion rings."

"The onion rings came l-later. The name came from the five rings they w-wore."

"So, what happened to the plaque?"

"It's b-behind one of the posters at the f-f-front, behind the r-r-register."

"I've never seen it."

"There's no real r-reason f-f-for you to. Well, not y-yet anyway."

"I'm sorry?" Lucy looked at the man.

"When the f-five men retired they made an agreement. They w-would never sell the business."

"Never sell it?"

"*Never.* They could *give* their t-title and deed to anyone they w-wanted—a relative, someone they admired, and so on, b-but they could never sell it."

"Amazing."

"When it's time to pass the t-title and deed along, the owner puts their golden ring on one of the f-five pegs on the plaque, designated for that r-ring, in the p-presence of the other owners. After shaking each h-hand of the other owners they take the ring off of the p-peg and slip the ring on the finger of the newly chosen owner."

"Incredible. So, they have an entire ceremony?"

"Yes."

"This is really amazing. Thank you so much for showing it to me. I'm sorry. I never did find out your name?"

"I'm William. William Muscalani."

"Well, Mr. Muscalani, thank you for showing me this."

The man smiled, nodded curtly, and walked slowly to the front of the diner, then turned to face Lucy. "You know, you r-really should see it."

"What's that?"

"The plaque. It's j-just b-behind that poster." He pointed to an old Chicago travel poster behind the register where Florence usually sat.

Lucy took down the poster and saw a beautiful dark oak plaque and five stubby pegs with brass plates and names under the diner's logo. "Oh wow!"

"Would you read the n-n-names to me? It's been a long time."

"Okay, let's see. There's Giorgio Muscalani 1919-1941, Johnny DeLuci 1919-1942, Randal Zacara 1919-1942, Dilan Watts, 1919-1943, and Moshi Finkelstein 1919-1944."

"Yes, the original f-five owners. Now the next row."

"Let's see, there's Billy DeLuci 1942-1961, Gabriel Muscalani-George 1941-1967, Betsy Zacara 1942-1955, Bill Finklstein 1944-1967, and James Barlow 1943-1971."

Lucy turned to William and asked, "So who are the current owners?"

There was a knock on the front door of the diner and Lucy moved to it. It was her regular, Joe, wearing torn-up pants and an old jacket with a rucksack over his shoulder.

"Hi Joe. What's wrong?"

"Nothing's wrong, Lucy. Everything's right!" he smiled.

"I don't understand?"

"You will," he smiled at her.

"I'm sorry, Joe, but we're closed. It's the holidays." said Lucy, as an apology.

Three cars pulled up to the curb, one parking behind the other and four people got out.

"It's alright, Lucy," came a familiar raspy voice. "Joe can come in."

"Florence? What are you doing here? I thought you were..."

"These are friends of mine and," Florence cut Lucy off and came through the door in a Christian Dior original, looking like a million bucks. "We're here to have a little party of sorts."

"Wait a minute, you look..." Lucy realized it wasn't her place to comment on Florence and started to walk to the back of the diner. "Oh, all right, I'll get my coat and take off then."

"Where do you think you're going?" Florence stepped in front of Lucy.

"I'm, I'm going home. I have to be back tomorrow night to close."

"No, my dear, I don't think you understand. You're *invited* to the party."

"But Florence..." she leaned in and whispered. "... I'm not *dressed* for a party."

"Trust me, dear. You look fine."

Florence led the way in, through the diner door. "Hello William, dear. How are you?" She went to William and kissed him sweetly.

"I'm better n-now that you're here."

"Oh, you tease!" she put her hand on his chest. "You just saw me at home."

"Wait a minute," said Lucy, "you two are…"

"M-Married, yes. Have been since 1966."

"Hello, Lucy, may I come in?"

"Judy? What are you doing here?" Lucy hadn't seen her since the night of her anniversary and the explanation of her husband's death.

"Yes, yes of course!" said Florence walking to her and giving her a hug.

Lucy stood to the side of the door with a confused expression and her mouth silently open.

"I hear there's a party in there!" came a voice from outside, white cane tapping the door frame.

"Chet?" Lucy was starting to get a little dizzy from all the strangeness.

Lucy went to Chet to assist, but he already had an escort; the lawyer that had made her life a living hell.

"Oh, hello," said Lucy a bit taken aback.

"Hello, Lucy," the man said with a very sincere smile.

"Jerome. Jerome DeLuci." He stuck out his hand for her to shake.

She took it, as a puzzled look crossed her face. "DeLuci. I know that name, but I can't place from where?"

"He's, my son," said Chet, taking a single step toward them.

"Your…" Lucy hadn't noticed the resemblance until that moment. Jerome was still smiling at her as he held her hand.

"Yes, Lucy, I'm his son. And, I have an apology to make to you I'm afraid."

"Oh?"

"Yes. I was a total ass to you and the staff the last few months."

"Oh? I hadn't noticed," Lucy lied.

"Yes! Yes, you were!" added Florence. "I should have thrown you out," she laughed.

"Yes. You should have," he laughed back. "But I had to be sure."

"Sure?" asked Lucy.

"Yes, Lucy. Sure." He retracted his hand and went to his father's side.

"Y-You see Lucy, w-we have a v-very special Christmas gift to give y-you."

Lucy's brow furrowed unconsciously. "Gift? What gift? For what?"

"Maybe I can try to explain?" Joe came out of the rest room wearing a suit as expensive as Jerome's with his face and hands washed and his hair combed and clean.

"Joe! Where did you get that suit? Take it off *right now* before you get in trouble!"

There was a moment of silence before everyone burst into laughter.

"Lucy, dear," Joe took her hand. "Let me properly introduce myself, I'm Joe, Joe Finkelstein." He waited for recognition, but it didn't come. He took her to the plaque on the wall and pointed. "Bill Finkelstein was my father."

Lucy finally understood where she had seen the name before. "Then you're…"

"Yes, Lucy," said Chet. "Billy Deluci was my father."

William took a step forward. "And Gabriel Muscalani-George was my F-Father."

"And Betsy Zacara was my mother," said Judy.

Florence moved to Lucy and put her hands on her shoulders, "and James Barlow was my papa."

Lucy looked into Florence's smiling eyes questioning why all the founder's progeny were in the diner.

"I'm sorry, I still don't understand why I'm here."

"Lucy, my dear Lucy," Florence lifted a hand to Lucy's cheek. "You don't know because we've kept a great secret from you until we were all sure."

Judy came to Lucy and took her hands, bringing her to the plaque. "Honey, you like this diner, don't you?"

"Well, yes, of course."

"Good. And William told you of tradition? The, uh… giving the deed of the diner to a worthy recipient?"

Lucy nodded.

"Good. And did he also tell you that the title and deeds are passed on to a new owner in a ceremony on Christmas Eve?"

"Christmas Eve?"

"Yes, Christmas Eve. In the past, the title has passed to an owner's progeny. Or if they didn't have children, someone worthy who's worked in the "Five Golden Rings;" someone who'd continue the original owner's vision. A place where *everyone* was equal, prince or a pauper, it didn't matter. A place you'd always be treated with courtesy and respect."

"From a bum," smiled Joe.

"To the blind," said Chet, raising his dark glasses to show cataract covered eyes.

Judy slipped off a ring and looked at it, "When it was time to pass on the restaurant, the owner would take off their ring and put it onto the peg under the original owners name." With a shaky hand Judy slipped the ring onto the peg under Randal Zacara's name plate. "Then they would give a hug of farewell to each of the owners in the room." Judy went to Joe and wrapped her arms around him for a long tearful time, then went to Chet, William and Florence in turn.

After, she turned and went back to the plaque. "The person who *was* the owner, now goes back to the ring on the peg and takes it down for one last time." Judy bore the ring in the palm of her hand and stood before Lucy, with a large smile on her face, and tears making her eyes sparkle. She took Lucy's left hand and silently slipped the ring onto Lucy's finger.

Lucy's furrowed brow eased and her eyes widened as she blanched in realization.

"No."

"Yes."

"No, no, no, no, no... This can't be happening."

"Oh honey, I assure you, it is."

"But you're... you're giving me one-fifth of the diner. I barely know you! How could you know..."

"Honey, I knew the first time you waited on me," smiled Judy.

"I'm sorry?"

"I knew the first time you waited on me. I came in four or five years ago every day for a week and watched everyone here. You were on top of it, smiling even when you didn't feel like it and, you knew your business. You were honest and looked out for the welfare of everyone, not just the people in your station. But, most of all," Judy pointed an arthritic finger at Lucy. "You were *courteous* when you didn't need to be. That's a trait no one can train. That's a natural-born gift from God. So, I give you my share and wish you a very Merry Christmas!"

Judy gave Lucy a long, tight hug. The hug made Lucy realize that this *was* real.

Then... it happened. Joe, Chet, William and Florence all went to the plaque, each taking off a ring at the same time and sliding them on their ancestor's corresponding pegs. After embracing one another, they came to Lucy and hugged her as the fifth owner, returning to the plaque and the four rings dangling there on their pegs. All four retrieved the rings and surrounded Lucy.

"Wait! Wait, you can't all... This can't be poss..."

Joe stepped forward and caught her hand. He didn't make a speech. He quietly slipped the ring on one of her fingers. Lucy's eyes filled with tears and her lower lip began to quiver. Joe led her to Chet who felt the air for her hand. Joe put Lucy's hand in Chet's and followed Joe's lead, sliding the ring on a finger.

William approached her next and with a slight ceremony, raised the ring for the former members to see. He then slipped it on her finger with a grand smile and drew her to Florence.

Florence tried to be the one stoic in the room but, as she brought the ring up to Lucy's finger, tears began to flow. Lucy couldn't take anymore and was crying in earnest.

"I... I don't know what to say," she whispered to Florence.

"Thank you usually works, dear," she smiled through the tears.

Lucy threw her hands around Florence and sobbed, "Thank you!"

After a minute of free-flowing tears, Lucy looked up to all gathered. "Thank you. Thank you all. It's, it's overwhelming and totally unexpected."

Jerome approached her and shook her hand with both of his. "Congratulations, Lucy. You deserve it."

"I'm not sure of that," she said, trying to dry her face with the heels of her hands.

"I am. I put you through the paces before I signed off my inheritance." He chuckled and handed her a pressed, starched handkerchief.

"Oh, no!" Lucy hadn't thought of that.

"No, no! This *is* the right decision. We all agree." He took the handkerchief and dried more of her tears, then handed the handkerchief back to her. "The five of them all chose you because you were the only choice that they all agreed on. I sure as hell didn't want anything to do with the restaurant business." Jerome chuckled. "I'm one of the highest paid lawyers in Chicago. And well, you're a very special woman, Lucy. I now see what they have for some time." He lifted his right hand and pointed around the room, "This world isn't for me, but you're perfect for it. So, when the time comes, and you know it's right, pass along your good fortune to others. But always remember, it's your courtesy to those that don't always deserve it that makes you special."

Each of the previous owners hugged Lucy at the door as they bid her 'farewell,' accompanied by another round of smiles and tears. This early Christmas Eve morning gift would be etched in her memory forever. The last person to leave was Florence.

"Now I expect you'll want a little training on the register tomorrow."

"Register? Me?"

"Well, if you want to do it."

"But that means…" Lucy suddenly looked sad.

"My dear girl," Florence took Lucy's hands. "Everything in this world changes."

"But…"

"No. No 'buts.' There aren't any 'buts' in this. The register is yours. Guard it well. Besides, I'm ready for some time off, and well, you have a new padded seat to break in!" Florence hugged Lucy one last time. "Consider this my two weeks." They both laughed.

After the hug broke, Lucy asked, "But what will you do?"

"Are you kidding? William and I are filthy rich! We're doing a yearlong world tour that starts in a month! You'll find out how much this place *really* makes. But it only works if no one knows you're the owner, so shh… okay?"

Lucy smiled. "Okay."

"Well, good luck!" Florence went to her waiting car and waved as she got in. "I'll send you a postcard!"

As Florence's limo started away, a police car pulled to a stop in front of the diner, and the window rolled down. "Miss? Are you open by any chance? Look, I know its past closing, but I'm draggin' and could really need a cup-a-Joe."

Lucy smiled at the officer and said, "Yeah, I think I can find a cup for ya. Come on in."

"Aw, thank you miss! You're a *life* saver!"

As the window of the patrol car rolled back up, Lucy heard over the police car's radio, 'Seven swans a swimming... Six geese a laying... Five Golden Rings...'

SIX GEESE A LAYING

Six Geese a Laying

A weather-worn man closed the cabin door and hobbled to an old wooden table before he lit the hand-rolled cigarette in the flame of the kerosene lantern. "So, your Pas sent ya up the hill to see your ol' Uncle Clayton, huh? Well, I 'spect they want me to tell ya bout the old days up here in the 'Laska Territory." He shook his head as he smiled at the four children sitting around the table, the early spring Northern Lights' bright-colored ribbons danced and swooped in the sky that peeked through the window behind him. Over his shoulder was a picture of twenty or more men—some with long beards, others clean-shaven—all carrying shovels, axes, and pans, wearing boots, coats, and snowshoes. He turned around and pointed to three men in the lower right of the picture.

"Now, this here, the one in the seal-skin coat, that's Rasmussen. I think he's Pa to a couple of ya. And that one there, in the black slicker, that there is Peters. That'd be the Pa to the other two of ya. And this here good-lookin' specimen of a man, well, that there, is yours truly."

A towheaded boy of about ten asked, "Where was that picture taken?"

"That was up in the Klondike, I'd say 'bout 1897 or 8."

"That was only fourteen year-a-ago." said a little raven-haired dark-skinned girl of about eight, dressed in buckskin and wearing a totem around her neck.

"Mr. Clayton, sir," asked a polite little red-headed waif of a boy. "Um, in the picture, sir, well, ya got two legs. How'd, well, how'd you lose one?"

Clayton Johnson sat back and took a deep pull on his cigarette and the ember glowed. "Well now, I'd figured your Pa's had told you that tale."

"No sir," said the redhead. "Pa told us ta ask ya when we saw ya."

"Well now, your Pas and I left San Francisco and quickly realized we were a good fit. So, we decided to stake a claim together and split everythin' we found up there three ways. After several weeks trekkin' through the ice and snow up to the Klondike, we needed to rest a spell and stock up on supplies. The three of us figured we'd do some trappin' and huntin' for furs and meat and come back together a few days after the full moon at the fork of a river. We each made way in different directions, Peters to the South, Rasmusun to the West, and I set out to the North.

"I did pretty well for the first week or so. It was May and I found a lake just east of the river where the snow had melted on the sunny side. I set traps and made a little fir tree bough shelter, then waited. I didn't shoot my rifle too often; I didn't wanna scare off the mink, beaver, and sable. And boy, did I get a lot of them. Hell, if we weren't headed for the Klondike, I'd of stayed and just trapped for a livin'. After I dressed the critters, I'd cook up some of the meat and put it in a bag, then hoist it up a tree so the bears and wolves wouldn't get to it. Then strip the fat off a the skins and let 'em freeze up flat so I could stack 'em and pack 'em.

"Well, about the second week, I stumbled on a goose that had its left foot caught in the crotch of a fallen dead limb."

"Did ya eat 'im?" asked a little four-year-old girl.

"No sweetie," Clayton chuckled. "I didn't. I was only eatin' the animals I was furrin'. Besides, there wasn't much meat on that ol' gander. No, I saw his leg was broke from a distance and slowly tried to creep up on him. Well sir, as I got closer, the gander's mate began to flap wildly, and honkin', and hissin' at me. I guess I would too if I thought my mate was gonna get eaten.

"Well now, I said, 'There, there little mother. Nothing's gonna happen to him.'"

"Ya talked to the goose?" asked the little four-year-old, eyes as big as silver dollars.

"Yes sir, I did. And it seemed to work. I told her, 'I just need to free him and see how bad the leg is broke.'" Well sir, for a time she calmed down. But when the gander started a raisin' a ruckus, she began to attack me with her beak snappin' and hissin'. So, I wrapped my arm with my coat for her to bite on while I eased out the gander's broken leg.

"I picked him up and took him to a nearby rock outcropping, layin' him on it gently. I told him, 'Let's see the damage, my friend.' I saw the leg was broke, but no bone was stickin' through, so I splinted it with an old red bandana and three short twigs. After that, I put him on the water's edge and backed away good and slow, then sat down against the rock, tellin' him, 'All right poppa, let's see how that works.'

"After I cleared away, he flapped his wings and rose enough to gently walk on the splinted leg. Well sir, soon as he was a flappin,' his goose flew down to him and nuzzled up close, windin' her long neck around his, first one direction and then the other. In a couple minutes, the gander clacked his beak nice and loud, and from around some reeds, six downy gray heads appeared. They were a swimmin' to their father as fast as their little legs could pump. Once safe to shore, the balls of fluff popped up onto the bank and waddled in a straight line to their momma and poppa.

"That's when something peculiar happened. I was about to stand when the goslings made their way to me. I didn't want to spook 'em, so I stayed sitting where I was. Each one of the goslings came to within three feet of my boots, looked at me a tiltin' their heads first this way, then that, then started sniffin me."

"Sniffin' you?" asked the towheaded boy.

"Sniffin' me like an old coon dog. Pretty soon, the mamma came up with the gander and they both dipped their heads to the ground and made a honk. Quick as a flash, mamma gave another honk, and 'splash,' they were all back in the water. I tell ya, one of the strangest things I'd ever did see."

"So, what happened to my Pa and old man Peters?" asked the redhead.

"Well, after another week and a half, we met back up by the fork in the river. They hadn't fared as well because they'd been huntin' with guns and scared all the game off. They'd just enough food to make it back to Skagway and figured they'd have to turn tail and go home with nothin' to show for it.

"I listened to their sorrows for a time and finally stood up, fetchin' six bags full of furs and another four bags filled with meat. Well sir, they couldn't believe their eyes. They congratulated me but continued to plan on returnin' to where they came from. I asked 'em, "Why are you still thinkin' about goin' home? There's more than enough here for all three of us to make it to the Klondike.'

"They couldn't believe their ears and said, 'It's your catch, we ain't got no claim to it.' I looked 'em both in the eye and said, 'We're a team ain't we? When we're up in the Klondike and Peters hits a big load, does that mean you and I are out of luck, Rasmussen? No! And what about if Rasmussen hits the mother lode with that big pick swing a his? Does that mean he's gonna leave us out in the cold, Peters?' Well, they looked at each other and as bold as you please, they slapped me on the back and shook my hand.

"We finally made it to the Klondike, and we dug in the cold ground and panned in the frozen streams. Did it for two years, collecting just enough gold to give us hope. I was all done, and one night sat Rasmussen and Peters down after supper and told 'em I was turnin' my part of the claim over to them. I'd make my way back to Skagway and work the docks until I had enough for passage back to San Francisco, and then home. They were sad but understood why I was leavin'.

"I took old George the mule. He was the oldest, lamest, and most obstinate of the pack and wouldn't be missed. After two weeks my provisions were gettin' a little low, so I thought I'd do a little huntin' and trappin'. I figured I'd sell the furs and get home even sooner. Well sir, I missed the signs of bear and wolves around the camp and hung the bear bag a bit too low to the ground, so when I came to get some vittles in the mornin', I saw a slash across the bottom. All my food had been torn open and et.

"I remembered a pond or lake not too far from that spot, so I packed my gear on George and made way to it. When I saw it, I felt in my bones there was somethin' special about the place but couldn't recollect why. I tied off George and began to set traps. After twenty minutes or so, I made way back to set up a small camp on the rise overlookin' the lake. Yes sir, that mornin' there was a slight glaze of hoarfrost, and the trees and bushes looked like they'd been covered in sparkling fairy dust when the sun hit 'em.

"Slippin' and slidin' my way over the slick reeds, I paused for a minute at the edge of the lake. Out of the corner of my eye, I saw a big momma grizzley that was out foragin'. I reached for my rifle and jumped up on a rock outcroppin' to get somethin' between me and her. That was a big mistake!"

"What happened? She take your leg?" came from the big eyed four-year-old.

"Ya see, I'd forgotten about the slippery hoarfrost on everythin'. I slipped off the rock faced down toward the lake. Well sir, I tumbled and broke my leg, then lodged my foot, almost backwards, in a crack in the rock. I dangled there like a piece of bait meat. My rifle had fallen to the flats, down by the lake, and I was in a pickle."

A general chorus came from all the children of, "Whoa!" and "Geeze!" and "Oh no!"

"Yup, that bear saw me fall, and of course, grizzleys being grizzleys, thought she had herself an easy meal. She came closer and closer, sniffin' the air around me.

"Yes sir, I thought it was the end and began to make peace with the Creator. The bear smelled the rifle and took a swipe at it, sendin' it flyin.' It got wedged between two loose rocks, and the bear got curious, comin'in for a closer look. Momma bear took several sniffs and put her four-inch claws on the barrel sticking up. When her paw slid down, a claw caught on the trigger. *BOOM!* It went off with an echo. The noise scared her, and she took off runnin'!

"The downside was ol' George was spooked, too. I don't know…the shot, the bear, the weather… Who knows? All I do know is he tore his mount from the tree and took off lickety-split back up the trail toward the great slope. So now we have the bear going in one direction, and George goin' in the other, and me a hangin' there from a trapped leg. Things looked pretty grim indeed!

"I managed to get my body propped up onto a small ledge, so I wasn't upside down no more, but couldn't get my foot free, it was wedged too deep, and was turned backward. I tried and tried to get free, but the more I tried, the deeper it got caught. Eventually, I passed out from fatigue. When I woke, it was the middle of the night, and I was terribly cold. The only good part of the cold was it made my leg totally numb.

"At dawn, I was surprised to see a 'V' of six geese comin' in for a landin' on the lake. They seemed to glide in so graceful like, with their feet tilted upward and their legs dangling straight below them. When they hit the water, it sprayed up like a stone skippin' across a pond.

"Not havin' much energy anymore, I went back to sleep and dreamed of scary and gnarled things; ropes and thorns stickin' and bindin' me. I woke with a start, not rememberin' what happened, that is, till the pain brought me back. I looked over the edge of the ledge and saw somethin' move just below me to the right of the lake. It looked like a goose was comin' out of the water staring up at me.

"The bird came closer and closer and tilted its head lookin' at me. A good share of the mornin' passed and one goose after another came up to take a look at me danglin' there. Eventually the largest goose began to flap her wings and landed just out of reach above me on the top of the out-croppin'. She made her way down from the top of little crumbly ledge to little crumbly ledge, to where I lay, and inspected me. She sniffed at me and gave a little honk. I looked right into her piercin' black eyes. Then, she opened her wings and silently glided back to her friends in the pond.

"A while longer, I heard a kerfuffle of clackin' of beaks and small honks and hisses. All at once, the gander let out a trumpet call toward the lake. It was loud and clear and a few minutes later I spotted a "V" of six more geese comin' in for a landin'. Then, not more than a quarter hour later, came a line of black-headed geese with white chests and brown coats swimmin' to shore; one by one, each approached the goose on land and the gander in the water, that had been standin' the semi-silent vigil.

"I got a cold chill and closed my eyes for a bit not knowin' if I'd wake up. I don't know how long I was out. I knew I was gettin' weak from the pain in my busted pinned leg. It may have been a day, maybe two. When I woke, the goose and gander were still there—the goose on land and the gander still in the water. I think the goose saw I was awake and flew up to just above me. There she sat, just lookin' down on me. She took a couple steps to her left and pushed at somethin' with her beak. The thing rolled toward me, stoppin' on the ledge above to my left shoulder. It was an off white very large goose egg! At first, I thought I was imaginin' things. It couldn't possibly be a goose egg. I had to be getting delirious after four or five days trapped with no food.

"I reached for it and stretched my stiff arm above my head. It was too far away. I tried to reach it the rest of the day, but no matter how hungry and how determined I was, the egg was still out of reach. Due to fatigue, I fell back into a deep dreamless sleep.

"When I woke up, I knew I was almost out a time. The world was dimmer, and colors weren't as vibrant in the sun. I couldn't focus my mind or eyes for more than a few seconds without driftin' off again. I glanced up where the egg was, but now saw two! I didn't know if I really saw them, or if it was a mirage.

"With a dyin' man's determination, I reached up and finally got one egg in a shakin' hand. I couldn't believe my luck and cracked the egg then sucked out the rich white and yolk.

"When I ate the egg, the gander let out a trumpet call below. He spread his wings and begin to flap wildly. I honestly didn't know if he was doin' it as a defense or as a morbid congratulations, but I quickly got the other egg and ate it hungrily. The next mornin', I woke to another egg, this time even closer to my head on the ledge. I looked down and saw my sentry had not left his post. I told him, 'I'm truly sorry about eatin' your kin in front of you. But I thank you and your brood for your kindness. You've saved my life, as little as it's worth right now.'

"Later that day, I woke to a new feelin' of pain in the leg, and it smelled sorta sweet and sour, like spoiled meat does. I thought, *Oh no, that's gangrene.* I knew I was in even worse trouble. After passin' time between fallin' asleep and chills with fever, I could feel things in my leg changin'.

"On the eleventh or twelfth day, I looked down for the gander and his family, but he was gone. I felt totally alone. I heard somethin' scratch just above me and looked up. There he was, on the ledge right above. It was the first time I'd seen him outta the water. He was sittin' there, silent, watchin' me with those sharp, jet-black eyes. And that's when I noticed it. The gander had the remnants of a red bandana wrapped around his left leg. It was pretty torn up and most of it gone but, it was there.

"I tilted my head back and saw that one of the geese had left me another egg present. This was number six, in as many days. I looked back to the gander starin' at me with his right eye and said, 'I wouldn't blame you if you didn't want to watch.' I cracked the egg, and he began sweepin' his wings back and forth, creatin' a low rumble; he began to clack his beak quickly, makin' a rapid tattoo, almost in tribute to the sacrifice of kindness to this human.

"The next day, the poison from the gangrene had started gettin' into my bloodstream and the smell was gettin' much worse. I knew if somethin' didn't happen in the next two days, I'd be dead and tried to move my foot again, but it was no use. Then I felt another set of eyes on me.

"I looked down and saw a lone she wolf's a movin' in my direction, nose high in the air. She moved in closer and closer until she looked up and saw me layin' there, just waitin' to be taken down like a wounded moose. She sprang for me and almost got me on the first jump, but I was a bit higher, and she skidded back down the rock face to the ground. I knew my luck wouldn't last, and she'd find the distance and pull me, part by part, off the ledge.

"I saw the wolf crouch just below and gave my gander friend a slight smile saying, 'Goodbye old friend. Thank you for your kindness.' Then I closed my eyes and waited for the end to come.

"I heard a low rumble come from above me and felt a breeze. I opened my eyes and saw the belly and legs of the gander a flyin down over me, right at the springin' wolf. The gander's beak caught the wolf right on the nose, and the wolf pulled up short, a bouncin' off the rock wall, only eight inches below my danglin' leg.

"The wolf scrambled to its feet, and the gander put itself directly between me and the wolf. She charged at me again. This time the gander tried to attack the wolf from the side, crashin' into her left. The collision was just enough to throw off the wolf's line, and it smashed nose-first into the ledge to my right.

"I saw her eyes. She'd decided to kill the gander, then come back for me. I was powerless to stop it and tried yellin' at the wolf. That wasn't workin' so I looked at the gander, barkin'. 'Fly! Leave me! Git! Ya got a family! Go on!' But he was more stubborn than I was and stood his ground. The wolf moved so the gander was cornered, not enough room to spread its wings and fly away, even if he wanted to.

"Things started to go all wonky in my eyes. I started seein' little white stars and a real high-pitched squeal blasted in my ears. The white blanks in my eyes spread and all went black. My vision left first, and I heard a loud 'pop' sound, before I faded away and didn't hear or see anymore."

Clayton stopped talking for a minute and poured a little whisky into a grainy see-through glass, filling it about half-way before stopping. He put the cork back in the bottle and held the glass up in a toast to the picture of his friends behind him.

The dark-haired and dark-skinned little girl tugged on Clayton Johnson's one pant leg. "Mr. Clayton, Mr. Clayton, what happened?"

"I woke up two weeks later lyin' in the back of a sled feelin' terrible. I was still sweatin', but I was alive. I opened my eyes and looked up into the smilin', but worried, faces of Rasmussen and Peters.

"Well now, look who's back, Peters! Looks like Clayton's back in the land o' the living."

"You've had two weeks of lollygaggin' around here. No more gold brickin' for you, well…"

"Rasmussen dipped his fingers into the black bush he calls a beard and scratched, smiling,"

"Not unless ya plan on helpin' us carry 'em all outta the Klondike, that is."

They both smiled big grins and Rasmussen started to laugh, 'We did it! We did it! We hit a big strike!' I couldn't believe what I heard. I thought I was dreamin'. 'You what?' I asked. 'We hit a big strike,' Rasmussen said while he was shakin' my arm. I started feelin' pain from just below my knee and tried to look down there. 'Yeah.' Rasmussen said, his bushy eyebrows knit together in a scowl. 'To get you outta that spot you were in we sorta had ta cut your leg off.' Then he smiled a big grin again and said, 'But you're 'bove ground, and ain't wolf bait no more.'

"Peters joined in, 'Yeah, it were a real mess, that leg a yours. It were et up clear through to the bone. Weren't no good no more anyhow."

"I had to know what the hell happened to me and asked 'em, 'What took place out there? How'd ya find me? The last thing I remember was a wolf jumpin' at me like a bag of bait.'

"They looked at each other and Rasmussen lifted off his hat and scratched his head, sayin,' 'Well, we hit the load a couple days after ya took off down the slope. We spent a couple more a days diggin' and rootin' around and decided to take our haul in, to the settlement to get 'er weighed up. After we got the first load out, we realized that we were diggin' in *your* spot. Well, we sorta talked it over and said it were only right that you'd still be a part a what we got, since we wouldn't a got up there in the first place if it wasn't for ya a bailin' us out on the way up...' then Peters broke in, "So we struck out down the slope after we secured things and ran in to ol' stubborn George. He was a eatin' some fresh growth. Well, we figured that you were stoppin' to provision up before ya went down the second slope, and we remembered ya went North when we went the other ways.'

"Peters rubbed his face the way he always does when he's thinkin', and said, 'That's when it got a bit strange. We heard a goose a honkin a storm. We came a runnin' and saw ya layin' high up and a wolf a springin' at ya.' Rasmussen jumped in, sayin', 'Yep, that goose was a flappin', and a honkin', and a carryin' on somethin' fierce. So, I raised my rifle and hit the wolf square in the back a the head. Killed um dead on the spot. Then we shinnied up on that rock and saw what happened. But before we could touch ya, that goose flew up n stood a hissin' and a flappin' up a breeze right over your head, like some kinda watch dog or watch goose or somethin'. We couldn't figure out what in blazes was a goin' on and tried ta shoo it away, but it wouldn't go. I pulled my pistol on it and started ta fire but... I stopped.'

"I asked him why he stopped, and Rasmussen said, 'I remembered ya said somethin' bout mendin' up a goose foot with that ol' red bandana a yourn. I ain't super-stiches mind ya but, I'll be danged if that goose didn't have a strip a old red cloth on his bur. So, I put the pistol down and talked gentle-like to the goose, 'Hey goose, he's hurt bad and we're here ta mend him up,' and stuff like that. Well, I'll be dangged if that goose didn't stare right through me, then ol' Peters, and turned tail swoopin' down ta the edge a the lake. After that, we cut your leg off with one stroke. I tell ya, it was a thing a beauty. Never seen control like that before.'"

All the children reacted with "Ew... Oh no... Ugh...!"

"So, kids, that's the story of my bum leg and doin' somethin' kind to a feather creature that saved my life."

"Mr. Clayton, what's that up there?" asked the little blond boy, pointing at something shiny on the shelf behind Clayton.

He turned around and saw what the boy was pointing at and reached up, retrieving it. "Well son, that happens to be the first chuck of gold I pulled out with my own hands from the Goose Foot mine. Here son, take a look-see."

"Mr. Clayton, why is it shaped like a big egg?"

"That's not just any egg son, that's a giant goose's egg. I had it fashioned outta the chunk of gold and put on a stand. Then I had the inscription put on the stand base. Can ya read it in this light?"

"I think so."

"All right, go ahead then."

The boy cleared his throat and read, "Thanks to the red-gartered gander and his six geese a laying. Cause of your kindness, ya saved my life."

SEVEN SWANS A SWIMMING

Seven Swans a Swimming

When my human touches my head, I looked up at him and sigh. I like it when he pets me. My human's name is Lenny, at least, that's what others of his kind call him. He calls me 'Georgie.'

I'm the best herding dog Lenny ever had, and I know it. It's not bragging. It's something everyone knows. Australian Shepherds know how to read the minds of the herd and pick out the leader on sight. It's just fact. We're told by our elders when we're pups, we'll be battered, bruised, and kicked. It's all for the honor of being the best there is. But the key is to be obedient to your human, do more than what they ask, and they'll treat you the way we're supposed to be treated, like one of their family.

I'll be honest, in the last few years my joints have begun to ache. Especially when it's cold and damp in the field. But laying in front of a warm fire at Lenny's feet... well... I'm right where I've belonged every night for the last sixteen years.

For all this time, I've taken care of the herds for Lenny and his mate, Cassandra. But now, the tables have turned. Lenny is taking care of *me* more and more. He won't let me herd the sheep, cattle, or goats anymore. He thinks I'm too frail or old or something. No, my eyes and ears aren't as sharp as they once were, and when I crouch down to stare a ram into submission my joints lock and yes, it leaves me limping for the rest of the day. But it's what I'm meant to do! Sometimes, I don't think they really understand me.

These days I'm relegated to the house yard only. I get shooed outta the barn or field. I don't think they'll let me run things my way ever again. I've been about obedience my whole life—either insisting on it or giving it—but these days, *no one* listens to me. I'm the old man they want to put out to pasture.

My 'lead position' was taken over by a two-year-old Corgi named Lizzie, a something-doodle named Muffy, and a scruffy little terrier mutt named Bones. It takes all three of them to try to replace me, and honestly, they're bad at it. I mean it, they really stink! They're nowhere near as quick, or confident. But times change and my human's mate wants "cute dogs with a personality" on the farm—whatever that means. It doesn't matter to her if the job is done right or not, she just wants cute things around. Well, at least, that's what I think. I don't really speak human that well.

I admit it, I'm bored. I've been herding sheep, goats, and cattle in line my entire life. I'm not talking about three or four. No. I mean seventy, ninety, a hundred and sixty at one time. Now, my only excitement is watching squirrels do acrobatics on overhead lines and chickens peck at each other. Sometimes I might get to referee the ducks when they get in

a squabble. But that's not very often. I miss having a pur-
pose.

I did like watching Madge though. She was great. Madge
was the mother swan that lived from mid-spring to late fall
on the edge of the pond behind the house. She was the perfect water herder. Over the eight seasons she was here, I
watched her whip those baby swans into shape. I'd hang out
down there just to watch her work her magic. It was a mas-
terclass in instinct. She knew how the young brood would
react in any new situation; how they'd turn in a storm, rough
water, or even when faced with Simon—the local water
snake.

Now, I don't speak 'sheep,' 'human,' or 'swan' (well, I
know a few words and phrases in human, but they don't always make sense). No, I read the sounds and movements
mostly. Don't tell anybody, but I picked up a new technique
from watching Madge. She did this one move—raising up,
spreading, and fluttering wings fast... Well, I made it my
own, I do what humans call 'downward facing dog' then,
quickly spring up and kick my hind feet forward, right into
the face of a ram or lead ewe. Those little furry beasts would
be on guard from that point forward, wondering what I'd do
next! Priceless.

I'll never forget last year. It was early Spring, and I decided to go down to the pond to visit Madge and her cob,
Corry. Corry and Madge had been a pair for ten seasons and
were getting a bit long in the beak. When I got down there, I

heard a big commotion. Madge was out in the middle of the pond, swimming in circles around and around a white mass of matted feathers, her wings fluttering and her beak swinging and trumpeting. I thought I heard the peeping of a new brood, all squawking in a clump of cattails to my right.

Well, I plowed through the mud, plunging headlong into the water. Now mind you, I'm *not* a Labrador or a Retriever, but I can hold my own in the water. After an eternity, my muscles started to cramp up, but I went on. I finally got to Madge—wild eyes and flapping and bumping the lump of white with her chest. Then, I realized what it was. It was Madge's cob, Corry. He wasn't moving, wasn't breathing, just lying stone still. He was dead.

Madge did something she'd never done before—she hissed at me! I mean full on, "I hate you and the world, don't cross me, I'm scared…" hiss. Now I get it, she didn't know why I was there and was going to protect her mate with everything she had. But I swam to Corry anyway and gently wrapped my mouth around the base of his long neck.

Madge went wild! She began to peck and screech and jab at me; she took out some pretty big chucks of fur off my back. But I knew I was doing the right thing though and swam for shore with Corry in tow.

Once on the bank, I carefully nudged Corry's body up on to dry land and moved away so Madge and her cygnets could pay their respects. I hadn't seen the babies yet; I'd only heard them, but I knew their lives were all about to change, and I felt sorry for them, for all of them, but mostly for Madge.

▶◆◆◆◀

Two days went by, and I led Lenny to Corry's body on the shore. Lenny did a good thing. He took a spade and buried Corry on the edge of the pond, not too far from the weeping willow where Madge liked to relax. She spent every waking moment just offshore, for the next week, sitting and staring at the spot where Corry was.

About ten days later, Madge's cygnets went into the water. It was time for training, and they all followed her in a straight line, heading for deeper water and their first lesson in how to handle waves bigger than they could see over. I had to smile. I knew Madge had to be hurting, but she kept on moving obediently forward for her little ones like nothing had changed.

In reality, everything *had* changed. Madge wasn't taking care of herself, and it showed. Usually after the eggs hatched, Corry and Madge would share time watching over the brood so each could feed and forage on their own. Now, Madge was alone. Over the next half moon, Madge lost almost three eggs worth of weight, her eyes were dull, and she didn't seem to be as sharp as usual. She spent almost every night floating a stone's throw away from where Corry was buried. Then she would let out the longest most mournful trumpet call any swan has ever given.

I always watch for signs and then help, it's what a good shepherd does. I can tell when a young ewe is about to give birth or if they're in trouble. But this was different. I didn't know how to assist Madge. I mean, I have no experience with swans, let alone assisting one. But I knew a friend was hurting, and really wanted to help.

One day, I was sitting under the willow, wondering how I could be of service, when I saw the local coyote named Ausu move in on the nest. Madge didn't see his approach. The last time I'd seen Ausu, I remembered him being trained by a particularly brutal pack. Ausu was tricky. He'd trot by a victim, then suddenly turn and attack. I looked for other coyotes but didn't see any; it looked like Ausu was alone. When I looked back, he'd disappeared. The crafty little bugger had hid into the low reeds.

Well, my hackles lifted. I'd seen Ausu's aftermath on a couple newborn lambs, and I didn't like the coyote being so near Madge and the nest. I crept low and quiet to the swans, and it's a good thing I did! I saw him strike! Ausu wrapped his mouth around a nice fat cygnet and backtracked silently into the reeds. Madge must have sensed something was wrong because she stood tall and strong, trumpeting as loud as she could.

I caught up to Ausu in eight or nine strides and rammed headlong into his side. The jolt sent him tumbling over and over and the cygnet popped free from the dirty thief's mouth. By the time he realized what had happened, I was up, hackles at full attention and standing between Ausu and the cygnet, back arched, and focused on him.

Well, we're about the same size, Ausu and me, but I was puffed up, looking two times larger. Ausu had a surprised look in his eyes and warily slinked back into the reeds. Then I saw him climbing the far hill on the other side of the pond.

The poor little cygnet was petrified, so I gently brought him back to the nest and carefully laid the little fuzzball just outside Madge's reach, because I didn't know what she'd do to me. The last time we were close didn't go so well. I set him down and went to the edge of the reeds and sat a little way away.

Madge cocked her head one way, then the other, while standing in the nest, blinking her eyes in my direction. I think she was trying to figure out if I was a friend or still a danger. It didn't take her long to decide. She took a few steps toward me, dropped her head to the ground—almost bowing—and clattered her beak. I think it was a sign of regard or respect. Well, I cocked my head to the side, ears up, and waited to see what came next. When she didn't make any other move at me, I laid down and let out a little whine of "You're welcome." I think she understood me because Madge came closer. When she was within touching distance, she lowered her head to the side of my face and sniffed. I stayed stone still. I didn't want to spook her and waited to see what she'd do next.

She took me by surprise by wrapping her long neck around mine and rubbing up and down. The feeling of her long, muscular neck around mine, well, it made me feel good, cared for. It made me feel all warm and tingly, like when my human really shows he appreciates me.

▶◆◆◆◀

Through the rest of the summer, when I could sneak away, and after my human went to bed, I'd quietly go through the doggie door and spend the nights at the water's edge to keep watch over the nest. Ausu hadn't been spotted in a couple moons but, I knew he'd be back, this time with friends.

I got to know each and every one of the cygnets and I became their favorite dry land playground. They'd clamber up onto my back then slide down to the ground. They'd play hide-and-go-seek under my legs and tail, then weave in and out of my feet when I'd get up and stretch to take a walk.

As they grew and the fuzz turned to pin feathers, Madge would send them to preen me, just as they would each other. They'd close their sandy-edged toothless beaks over a clump of my fur, then gently pull back, cleaning away the mud and dirt, till it would be straight and shiny. I think it was a real honor. Either that, or I was really dirty!

With Corry gone, I'd sit as a sentry over the nest while she would go out to the middle of the pond. She'd tuck her head under her wing and catching a few winks. I think we both knew this would be the last summer of her having a brood on the edge of the pond. I mean, she didn't have a mate anymore, and swans' mate for life. When they lose a mate, they don't go back to the homes they created as a couple. I'm not sure, but I can imagine how heartbreaking that would be. So, we made the best of the days we had left together. It was a friendship that came late in our lives, but it came along at the right time.

One day, about four moons after my human buried Corry in the ground, I lay at the side of the pond, my head on the edge of the nest for a pillow. It was hot and the grasshoppers were rubbing their legs together in a low raspy wheezing while the meadowlarks called back and forth. The red wing blackbirds were whistling their song, and I was dozing when Madge gathered her brood of seven around her, mid pond. They had really grown and changed. Each one had their own personality and had become more white than gray.

She gave a loud pointed trumpet call and all seven flapped their wings together, testing them. They created enough breeze to start rings rippling in the water away toward the banks. After one more loud *honk* from Madge, all seven moved forward, leaning into the slight, hot breeze and they began to lift off the water. They looked like they were running across the top of the water! Then it happened—all seven lifted into full flight!

I couldn't believe it! I scrambled off the soft ground and sat, watching their maiden flight. I let out four or five sharp barks in celebration.

They were no longer in need of care and fully capable of flying away from danger. It was hard to accept but my time protecting the cygnets was at an end. A warm feeling washed through me, even though my life, our lives, would soon change. I felt real happiness watching the seven angle and spiral in the air, dropping ever so gently back into the water—feet out in front of them.

All seven swans were swimming back to the nesting area, chortling and clacking their beaks in celebration, while Madge slowly sailed to where Corry laid in forever rest. Back on shore there was honking and 'high fiving' of beaks. I couldn't help it, I barked and whimpered with joy.

Then it hit me. I felt out of place; like an intruder in this family gathering and thought maybe it best if I went back to the house. You know, to let them enjoy the things swans enjoy by themselves. My front right paw had fallen asleep. I turned and limped about ten paces toward the farmyard before being startled by a shadowy figure in front of me. There, wings fully outstretched, was Madge, flapping and shooing me back to the brood! She wasn't going to let me leave the bevy I'd helped guard and oversee. I've got to admit, I'd never felt so good, so cared about. I all but skipped back to the water's edge! I was welcomed and surrounded by the seven, all in turn wrapping their long and heavy necks around mine and tugging on my ears.

►♦♦♦◄

It was deep autumn when the seven young swans took flight from their home one last time and angled southward. Madge left the day after her young and looked back at me that morning. I'll never forget it. There was a slight mist wafting over the water as the sun began to rise. I got to the nest, and there, in the middle of the pond, in the very spot she'd last seen Corry alive, sat Madge. She turned her full body toward me one last time, dipped her head, and trumpeted loudly. I wanted to honor her and our friendship, so I bent my front legs until my chin came to the ground, sort of like what she did in the water.

With no warning, Madge wheeled around and in four flaps, lifted off the pond, banking in the same direction as her now fully grown children. I stood there watching as she slowly became smaller and smaller, until the pinpoint of Madge blended into the fiery orange and yellow sunrise. I said my goodbyes and made my way back to the house. I'll be honest, I didn't feel like eating for a couple weeks after they left. I felt… alone.

It's now spring again. Starting a few days ago, I've made way down to the pond, not expecting to see any of them return, but hoping—always hoping. I spend a good share of every morning there, but eventually, I get cold, and my joints ache, so I go back to the warm fire with my humans.

Day before yesterday morning, I got to the pond and suddenly felt a searing pain in my left flank and right of my neck. A cold shiver ran down my spine when I realized, I was being attacked by more than one set of teeth! I knew if I fell to the ground I'd never survive. Staggering, legs spread apart, teeth fully bared, I saw out of the corner of my eye Ausu, barking at his pack to bring me down. I fought harder, longer, and stronger than I ever had in my life.

I felt my front knee buckle, then the left rear give way. I was being pulled over by teeth between the shoulder blades, and behind my wet neck. I landed on the soft bank and felt the blood leaving my body. I knew that was it and prepared for the end. I closed my eyes, figuring Ausu's fangs were about to dig into me. I was facing the pond and away from the pack.

I started drifting away when I saw all seven of Madge's and Corry's young swimming toward me, necks outstretched and honking furiously with fire in their eyes. The last thing I saw was all seven, attacking the three coyotes—strong beaks hissing, slashing, and clamping down on any part of the coyotes they could reach. The pack tumbled over each other, retreating for the woods on the far side of the pond. I saw the coyote fur falling from the swan's beaks like hairy snow, hearing the loudest trumpet calls I'd ever heard.

I thought I was too far gone and tried to raise my head to whimper a '*goodbye*' but, all went black.

▶◆◆◆◀

I woke, lying in front of the place for fire and Lenny's stockinged feet in my face. I heard the human words, "I tell ya, it was the darndest thing! I came in from herding the sheep to the near pasture and I couldn't hear myself think from all the noise them swans were making down at the pond. There lays Georgie, in the middle of seven of 'em. There was blood and coyote fur everywhere. I really didn't think they'd let me anywhere near him, but as I came close, they opened up, like a big white doorway. I tell ya, strange."

Lenny looked down at me when I looked up at him. He reached down and petted my head, stroking it slowly, gently. He said, "There, there boy. You rest now."

I heard Lenny tell his mate as I was drifting off to sleep, "After I picked Georgie up and took him to the truck to go to the vet, I looked back at them swans. There they were—all staring at me—looking back at them. All seven swans a swimming, making sure that Georgie boy was going to be all right."

I fell asleep thinking, *All seven of MY swans a swimming. I'll keep watch over our family Madge, don't you worry.*

VIII

EIGHT MAIDES A MILKING

Eight Maids a Milking

The towering 5' 12" dark blonde strode past her office door with "Samantha A. Manfred" embossed on the sign and went straight for the boardroom at the end of the hall with *Smith-Harrelson-Woodbridge Brokerage Boardroom One* emblazed over it.

"Oh! Sam! How *nice* of you to show up for the meeting," sniped a slight woman, smiling in power suit and pearls, seated on the left side of the table surrounded by ten other people.

"Oh! Janice! It would have been *nice* of you to tell me you changed the time of the meeting *I* set up," Sam countered, voice as sweet as spiced honey. "*This* meeting. That *could* have been very collegial. Alas, I found out." Sam turned to Janice and smiled, "despite your *best* efforts," then turned away. "F-ing cow," she muttered.

"All right you two..." said a slightly overweight man in his mid-fifties wearing a $3,000 suit at the end of the table and a visitors pass around his neck that read, JAMES CHILDER – OWENS & CHILDER - MERGERS ACQUISITIONS. "And that goes for everyone in this room. Your company is in deep caca, and you have no paddle to stroke with. You called me in to bail your company out of this hostile takeover. So, I suggest you all go eat separately, calm down, and meet back here in two hours with ideas as to how to save your company. Clear? Good. Now, get out." He looked to the other side of the table, "All but Sam. Hang back, will ya?"

After the others had left, he said, "Why are you still here? You're too smart for these idiots. They'll be belly-up in three months."

"That long?" asked Sam with a wry smile sitting.

Childer tipped up a can of Diet Coke and drank to the end, then said, "Look, right now, this company's facing not just a poop storm, but a poop *hurricane*. I'll try my smoke and mirrors, then throw the pipe bombs if I need to, but it's done." He turned to her with a concerned face. "Look, let me ask you a question. Are you happy working with these idiots?"

"Ms. Manfred, a call for you?" tailed off Sam's assistant as she saw her sitting with Childer.

"Take a message." Snapped Sam.

"I, uh, I can't? She's insisting she speak with you?"

"Carol? What does she want?" It always bothered Sam that her assistant made everything sound like a question. Sam patted Childers arm and went to her assistant. "Who is it?"

"It's a Miss Almbridge? She said something about your Aunt Lulu passing?"

▶◆◆◆◀

Three days later Sam got into her rental at the Albuquerque airport and drove toward Raton, New Mexico. After the wake, funeral and burial, Sam was asked to stop by her Aunt Lulu's attorney's office on her way out of town.

"What do you mean she left me everything?"

"Just that. After your mother passed, she gave you a little bit of what she had, but the majority went to her sister, Lulu. Now that Lulu's gone, well, it's all yours. Both ranches and the one hundred and twenty acres on both properties. Oh, and all the livestock and..." The man looked down and cleared his throat.

"And?" asked Sam, not amused at the situation.

"And..." the man smiled up at her. "And the young charges assisting in the running of the ranches," then cleared his throat.

Sam didn't think she'd heard the advocate correctly. "The... the what?"

The lawyer closed his file and stood, offering an envelope across the desk. "This will explain everything. Now, I have another meeting across the valley, so I'm afraid I'll have to scoot." He stood and walked past her, all but running through his office door. "If there's anything else you need, just call me or ask my assistant. She'll be back later today."

"But what about..." Sam stopped mid-sentence. The lawyer had left, and she was all alone in the office.

Sam drove the sixty-five miles of highway and dirt roads to her Aunt Lulu's old ranch house thinking about her amazing ninety-seven-year life. Aunt Lulu had always been a control freak and was probably the most brilliant person Sam ever met. She was one of the few women that had worked as a scientist on the Manhattan Project and the production of the first atomic bombs, just down the road at Los Alamos. But, when the war had finished, instead of pursuing a career at Lawrence Livermore Laboratories, or teaching for University of California Berkeley, she decided to become a math teacher at the local high school in Taos and help on the family farm.

Halfway to the ranches, Sam realized she hadn't opened the envelope the attorney had given her. She pulled off at a farmstand on the side of the road and bought a basket of peaches, then sat behind the wheel, door open, and slid her finger under the envelope flap. She recognized her aunt's handwriting immediately and suddenly felt a sad connection to the scrawls on the page.

"My dear little Milkmaid," Sam stopped and took a deep breath. She hadn't thought of her aunt's nickname for her in twenty-five or more years. *"Funny how time slips away. The last eight years of talking to you made me realize I can do only one more thing for you. I can save you from being so angry and damned uptight all the time. You once asked why I didn't go to California and become a world-famous scientist. The real reason wasn't fear, or lack of desire. No. It was because I*

wanted to be happy. That's it. I just wanted to be happy. I had
helped design something that took a quarter of a million lives
in under two minutes. And I helped develop even more weap-
ons to take even more lives. I just couldn't deal in death any-
more. I needed life around me. And I needed to do something
good for others. I needed to dedicate the rest of my life to noth-
ing but that.

"*So, if you're reading this, that means I'm gone. And*
you're about to go to the ranches your mother and I ran. What
you don't know is we've been taking in girls from the reserva-
tion for the past twelve years and a few from off Res about four
years ago. These girls have nowhere else to go. Some have been
beaten, others abandoned. Some have had hard lives as four-
teen-year-old prostitutes, and others ten-year-old drug ad-
dicts. Your mother and I have been the only 'family' these girls
have known, and I'm asking you to take over."

Sam sat stone still and read, then re-read the letter that
far three times before she turned the page over. "What the
f...." passed through her lips.

"*I know you haven't been happy in San Francisco, and I*
know you left home in a huff. But I'm hoping you give the girls
a chance. They really are the family you never knew.

"*Listen my little Milkmaid, I know all this is a shock. I*
tried to get your mother to talk to you about it before she
passed ten years ago. But, well, you know how stubborn she
could be..."

"*She* was stubborn? She was nothing compared to *you*," Sam said under her breath.

"*Now, I know what you're thinking. You're thinking, 'How quick can I sell this place and never come back to New Mexico?' But it doesn't work like that. This place has been in your family, OUR family for six, now seven generations. You don't just sell that off. No. So, I want you to stay at the ranch for at least two weeks. After that, if you decide you have to sell, well, then by all means do it. But I want you to do all you can to keep your heart, mind, and soul wide open. Let the place speak to you.*

"*So, that's it. I wish you all of God's Blessings, and I hope you open your heart to your mamma's and my other family.*

"*God love you, as I love you, my little Milkmaid.*

"*Aunt Lulu*"

Sam sat in stunned silence for ten, twenty, thirty minutes, just staring at the vast, wide open sage prairie. Her mind and emotions were a whir and bounced between tears and remorse, to anger at the situation her aunt had put her in. She couldn't keep one thought for longer than a breath's length before it morphed into something else. Realizing she was baking in the New Mexico sun, she finally closed the car door and drove to her aunt's ranch house, past the eighty head of sheep, forty head of goats, and a hundred head of

Holstein cattle grazing in the pastures. The last time she drove this road was... She couldn't remember.

Sam got out of the car and walked toward the ranch house. It was over a hundred and thirty years old and hadn't had sprucing up in over fifty. The porch needed a total redo, and the roof had a definite swale. As she put her hand onto the handrail, it collapsed under her weight. "Just ducky..."

Sam knocked on the door and a young, short, stocky native woman came to the window. After seeing who it was, she smiled broadly and ran to the door.

"You're Samantha. Grandma Lulu showed us your picture and the articles written about you all the time." The girl put out a strong hand, "My name is Nachoka. Pleased to meet you."

Sam took the young woman's hand out of kindness.

"We thought you'd be here a while, so we made up Grandma Lulu's bedroom for you." Nachoka looked down for a few seconds, then said, "I guess it's *your* bedroom now."

"That's very sweet, thank you so much. But this is just a quick social call. I, I need to get back to San Francisco. We're going through a hostile takeover and..." Sam stopped short. She realized the girl of eighteen or so in front of her had no idea what a 'hostile takeover' or 'merger' was. "Well, I need to get back."

Three other girls stood behind Nachoka in the doorway, all trying to steal glimpses of the woman in the pointy shoes outside the door.

"Are you our new Grandma?" came a little voice from the back.

Nachoka didn't turn around but stared out into the pasture. "No, I don't think the pretty lady has time for us. She's too busy."

The comment all but broke Sam's heart. She grew up with girls like this. She knew what they had been through and what they would face if they didn't have someone to look after them, nurture them, show them that they were worth more. She had been looking at them through the eyes of an executive, living in an ivory tower in some far-off city. "Well, I'll tell you what, I'll stay for three days and see if I can get work done for San Francisco while I'm here. How does that sound?"

Nachoka's innocent face lit up with a bright smile and said something to the girls behind her. In a flash, three young girls ran past Sam and Nachoka to the car and started transporting bags into the house. After borrowing some rubber boots, she toured the barn and farmyard, still dressed in her 'city clothes.'

Once back to the house, Nachoka asked, "Grandma Sam, may we call the girls from the other ranch over to join us for supper?"

"What other girls?"

"The older girls in our family, the ones about to go out into the world, they live at your mother's house. We all try to get together once a week or when we have something to celebrate."

"Well then," said Sam. "Absolutely call them! I'd enjoy meeting everyone that lives here. Second, why are you calling me 'Grandma Sam?' I'm not *that* old!"

Nachoka looked down and then took a step closer to Sam, holding a cupped hand up so she could whisper in Sam's ear. "It's a name of honor. Only those we honor highly get the name Grandma or Grandpa."

Sam looked down at Nachoka's eyes, seeing only care and admiration in them.

That night there was a true feast with pork, beef, lamb, and chicken served in old Fiestaware bowls on the sideboard, with fixings for tacos and burritos. On a side table, by the large bay window that looked to the west, was an array of different cheeses, butters, and creams: all handmade right there on the ranch.

Sam glanced up at the back wall of the immense country kitchen and said under her breath, "They're still there." On it were seven pictures of seven different women, all sitting on the same three-legged stool and milking cows, goats, sheep...anything with four legs. The first picture was of Marianne Reames, who was Sam's great, great, great grandmother. In the picture, she looked to be in her 80s, but was probably only 40. The picture next to Marianne Reames was of her daughter, Gloriana. Gloriana had light hair, and dark eyes, with her right cheek buried into a Holsteins flank and milk jetting out of the teat. The next three pictures were a blur, and she knew one was Priscilla, another Phoebe, and another Paulette. The last two pictures were Aunt Lulu and Sam's mother—wearing a bright gingham dress, a handkerchief in her hair, and a smile from ear to ear. She must have seen this picture five-thousand times, but never really looked at it. She'd never caught that all the women were smiling. They all seemed really, truly, and authentically happy.

Sam went to the dairy table and took her first bite of cheese. "Oh my God! I'd forgotten how good Momma's cheese was."

"Thank you," came the small voice Sam heard before. "That one's mine."

Sam turned and saw a girl of fifteen turn bright red and look down at her feet.

"This is amazing! Really."

The girl just stood there, face down and swaying back and forth, hands tightly clasped behind her.

"What did you say your name was?"

"Abigale. Abigale Eaglespur."

"Well, Abigale, this is some of the best cheese I've had in years, and that's saying something."

Sam looked to her left. There was a girl of seventeen holding out a plate of pure white cheese to her.

"What's your name?"

"Lucy. Lucy Highhawk, and this is my brie."

Sam took a large scoop of the creamy white cheese and spread it thickly on a homemade piece of bread. The flavors burst on her tongue, and she began to salivate uncontrollably.

"Oh, my G…" Sam realized her mouth was still full and chewed quickly. "This is amazing, too!"

The rest of the night, Sam tried every cheese, butter, yogurt, and ice cream the girls had made while listening to the heart-wrenching stories, each telling what had brought them to the ranch. Lucy had been an underprivileged girl that not only needed a home, but a family. Abigail had been to prison and became "in the family way" when a guard there raped her. Upon release, her family would have nothing to do with her. She ended up putting the newborn up for adoption, never to see or hear of it again.

Story after story came out around the table that night from each of the eight girls seated there. As the night wore on, Sam came to find out that first her mother, then Aunt Lulu, had been contacted by the county and Native American Tribal Women's Council. The groups knew that Sam's mother and Aunt Lulu needed help on the ranches and were willing to make the two elder women guardians over their troubled girls.

It was a win—win for Sam's mother and Aunt Lulu. The girls helped to keep the ranch going; meanwhile, they had homeschooling and a loving family to be a part of. As a teacher, Aunt Lulu's house was also home for the younger girls. As they aged out of the system, they could move on to Sam's mother's house, three miles away, and live there until they made longer-range life plans.

"Well, I have to admit, I am very impressed by all that you've shown me. But I have to be honest, I'm not sure what my plans are," said Sam at the end of the night.

The girls got very quiet and began to clean the table in silence.

"Was it something I said?" asked Sam, a bit confused.

Nachoka sat next to Sam as the girls continued cleaning in silence. "Grandma Sam, the girls don't have anywhere else to go. I don't have anywhere else to go. And…" she looked up at Sam with wide eyes. "I didn't mean to put pressure on you. I just wanted to let you know why they are so quiet."

Sam couldn't help it, the name of honor *Grandma* always made her flinch. "No. No pressure," sighed Sam, rubbing her face with her hands. "But I think I'll turn in for the night. If that's all right?"

"Of course, I put your things in your Aunt Lulu's room. Please," Nachoka looked up into Sam's eyes. "Please forgive me. I didn't want to make you feel bad by saying what I did. I meant no harm."

Until that moment, Sam had forgotten how naturally cheerful, gentle, and generous people can be. "Please Nachoka, know I have no ill will or bad feelings toward you, or what you said." Then Sam looked up at all the girls cleaning. "Good night girls, and thank you."

Each one of the girls stopped what she was doing, turned to Sam, and nodded respectfully and silently.

Two hours later, Sam was awakened by a beautiful three-part girl's chorus singing in the distance. She quickly pulled on sweats and went out the back door to a small fire ring down the hill from the house. At a distance, Sam saw all the girls standing around a dying fire pit, singing a beautiful, yet mournful tune. As the song came to an end, the girls hugged each other. The younger girls came back up to the house, the older girls got in a van and drove back to the other ranch.

Over the next three days, Sam spent four or five hours cursing and sputtering over the reports she'd received from San Francisco. On the fourth day, she took a long walk around the ranch yard and pasture, wearing a cobbled-up outfit of designer blouse, jeans, and old rubber boots, she'd come back calm and refreshed. She hadn't felt this way in a long, long time. Things were clear, balanced, right. She walked into the barn as a girl of twelve was hand-milking a ewe.

"It's Nalala, isn't it?" asked Sam.

"Yes, Grandma Sam," said the girl, her cheek planted against the sheep's side. "I'll try to be out by late tomorrow, but I haven't found anyone to milk my sheep yet."

"Why on earth would you be out tomorrow?"

"Word is you're selling the ranches."

"To be honest, Nalala, I don't know what I'm going to do." Sam realized she meant that in more than one way. "So please, you and the girls stay and do what you've been doing. This is still your home."

Nalala looked up for the first time, tears in her eyes, and a broad smile. "Really? We're not getting kicked out?"

She looked into the girl's face and it about broke Sam's heart. "Of course not! Where did you get that idea?"

"Well, Grandma Sam, we hear you talking all fancy to the people in San Francisco, and well, it seems like you'd rather be there, with the fancy people, then way out here in the middle of nowhere with us."

The comment stung Sam to the heart and she flinched. She remembered the last time she'd seen her mother alive, telling her, *"Why would anyone want to stay out here in the middle of nowhere with people like you?"*

"Nalala, may I ask you something?"

The girl stopped milking and turned toward Sam, giving her full attention.

"Nalala, I've heard you and the other girls sing a beautiful song down at the firepit every night after supper before the other girls go back to the other house. What does it mean?"

Nalala blushed and looked back to the sheep in front of her. "It's an old tribal song."

"What does it mean?"

Nalala sat silently for a long time then quietly said, "It's sort of a prayer to the Great Spirit. It talks about how thankful we are for all that the Great Spirit has given us, and that we are a family, no matter where or when we are on earth or in time... That no matter who makes us part from each other..." Nalala stopped and looked with fear at Sam, like she'd said the wrong thing.

"I understand," said Sam. "Please, don't worry. Keep telling me what it says."

Nalala looked away again. "It says, 'No matter who makes us part from our home, our sisters, our grandmothers, we are family forever. Bound. Sisters, mothers, granddaughters forever.'"

Sam hadn't realized it, but she had a single tear running out of the corner of her left eye. "Thank you Nalala, for telling me."

Nalala silently nodded and went back to milking.

►◆◆◆◄

Sam had a sleepless night. She went down to the kitchen and sat with a glass of fresh milk, looking up at the seven pictures of the women who lived and worked this ranch before her staring back down on her from the wall. Her mind was full of PR firms and advertising campaigns and profit margins. It wouldn't turn off no matter how hard she tried, and she felt her pulse in the red zone and couldn't get it to drop. After looking at the seven matriarchs for ten minutes and drinking the fresh milk, she suddenly felt sleepy and trundled back up the stairs to the big bedroom on the east side of the house.

In the morning, she woke to voices in the kitchen and heavenly smells rising up the stairwell. When Sam came down to breakfast, Nachoka looked at her, then at each one of the pictures on the wall, and said impishly, "Hey everybody, quiet down for a minute. I have an idea. We all know Grandma Sam is a business leader, but can she milk a goat?"

Sam looked at the girl's smiles, all shining, sisters in arms. "I can milk anything you put in front of me!" She laced her fingers together and put her thumbs down like a pair of teats hanging from an udder. "I can milk a sheep, goat, cow… I could milk a sow if I had a mind to."

The girls began to laugh and clap, chanting, "Prove. It. Prove. It. Prove. It…"

"All right, all right…" said Sam with her hands in the air trying to regain quiet. "Follow me." She went out the screen door to the milking parlor followed by all the girls, all but Nachoka, who ran upstairs to her bedroom to grab her camera.

"All right girls," said Sam loudly, pointing to the barns. "Go get whatever it is you want me to milk."

In a few moments, Abigale and Nalala led in a very large white, black-faced ewe in a harness. "This is Minerva," said Nalala.

"Here you go!" said Abigale, handing Sam a three-legged stool and stepping away.

Sam went to Minerva's head, looked her in the eye, saying, "Forgive me Minerva, for what I'm about to attempt. It's been a long, long, *long* time. Be gentle with me."

The girls laughed and Sam smiled as she went to take her place on the three-legged stool. Once perched, Sam laced her fingers together and cracked her knuckles like Liberace preparing to play a Chopin sonata. Slowly she placed her left hand then her right onto plump teats and began to squeeze, gently at first, then began to roll her fingers downward with a little tug. Within four motions, milk began to stream in hot jets.

The girls began to applaud and encourage both, Sam and Minerva. Sam was actually enjoying herself. She'd forgotten how satisfying the rhythm, the motion, and the sound were. She'd grown up on her mom's ranch doing this very thing day after day all the way through elementary school and early years of high school. After leaving the ranch for business school, she couldn't wait to drive away from the old 'dust hole.' But today, after the milking, the rest of her day was filled with reports, checking the Internet, making phone calls, and basically trying to create a plan. Sam began to realize how much she missed her younger, more carefree life in the 'dust hole,' and saw that she really needed the break from the crazy of the city. At least for now.

►◆◆◆◄

On night number seven of Sam being on the ranch, the girls threw a banquet in her honor. There was both lamb and brisket on the table, three kinds of corn, green beans, rolls and sliced bread, four different gravy boats filled to the brim, five kinds of potatoes, and four different bowls of greens. The dairy table had Gouda, Cheddar and Brie, with honey butter, orange butter, and salted butter, then five kinds of sliced bread. The tables were overflowing with food. But Sam knew nothing went to waste on the ranch. The girls from the other ranch would take some home, and the leftovers would be the base for the next three day's meals.

After supper, the girls invited Sam out to the fire ring for the first time and sang the tribal song of sisterly grace. Sam couldn't keep her façade any longer and tracks of tears streamed down her face unabashedly at the pure love that washed over her. She hugged each girl as they left the dying embers and decided to stay at the ring a little longer. As she stared into the glow, an inspiration spun itself into a thought, and then into a loosely formulated plan. She all but ran back to the house and looked at the contacts on her phone. She hit speed dial 'JAMES CHILDER – OWENS & CHILDER - MERGERS ACQUISITIONS' as the door slammed behind her.

"James? When was last time you had shit on your shoes?"

►◆◆◆◄

Sam pulled into the airport arrivals area at 6:22 am, tired but happy. There was James Childer on the curb, in a $1,000 pair of cowboy boots, new blue jeans, a designer snap-button shirt, and the silliest—and most expensive—straw cowboy hat she'd seen in years.

"Hey little lady! Wanna give a cowboy a lift?" he said, as he stuck out his thumb.

"Sure thing. When I find one, I'll be happy to!"

Back on the ranch Sam gave Childer the grand tour and unfolded her overall plan.

"See, I look at this place in several ways. First, it was my mom an Aunt Lulu's idea to have a refuge for girls that needed help. I think we take it a bit farther. We incorporate, then they learn a trade by working here, not just milking. But also, the bookkeeping, hospitality, packaging, distribution, you know… Everything about business from the ground up. As for formal schooling, a neighbor is a retired kindergarten through high school English teacher, and we have four other retired teachers wanting to sign on. They'll tutor and home school the girls, in exchange for cheese, milk, and yogurt."

When Sam took him in the house, the girls were hard at work setting up for lunch.

"Holy goat!" said Childer. "You guys eat like this all the time?"

Sam took him to a large refrigerator on the back wall of the kitchen. "All right, you've seen the general operation. Now you need to try the product."

"Don't mind if I do." said Childer, rubbing his hands together.

Sam brought out blocks of cheese, small, covered bowls of yogurt, Mason jars full of milk, and five tubs of butter.

"All right, start trying. Tell me what you think," Sam said, very businesslike, picking up a yellow legal pad and setting it next to him.

Childer sat on a bench seat, his back to the window, looking like a little mouse in a pantry with mounds of food all around. "I, I don't know where to start!"

Thirty minutes later, Childer pushed himself up from the bench with a pad full of notes and came into the office area where Sam was chewing on one of her cuticles.

"Well?"

Childer had a very serious look on his face, biting his lower lip.

"Well?"

He put his hands behind his back, walking in circles in the office, taunting Sam with silence.

"*Well?!*"

"I see..." he said, belching. "I see a lot of problems."

"Oh? Like what?"

"Like..." He walked to the other side of the room and ran his fingers over a stack of files.

"*Like?!*" Sam became insistent.

Childer put his big meaty left-hand out and began to enumerate on his fingers. "Like, you're going to need a bigger office, and a very, very large bank for all the money you're going to make." He then smiled a huge Cheshire grin.

Sam couldn't contain herself, jumping out of her chair and giving him a huge hug.

"Whoa, wait a minute now. We still have some issues to work through." He said seriously. "We have licensing, incorporating this as a 'learning institution,' and…" he stopped cold, looking up at Sam.

"What?" she asked, thinking the worst.

"What are we going to name this venture? I mean, 'Goat's Galore' or 'Sheep's Dip' just won't work. It has to be the right angle."

Sam scowled and walked back to the office chair.

"Grandma Sam?" Nachoka was at the door.

"Yes, Nachoka?"

"We, the girls and I, I mean, we made a dinner for you and Mr. Childer, and we, uh… we sort of have something to give you."

Sam looked at her watch. She and Childer had been at it all afternoon and now it was almost sundown. "Oh? What's that?" she said, standing to go into the kitchen.

"It's, well, it's out here." With a huge smile, Nachoka backed away and went into the kitchen.

When Sam and Childer entered the kitchen, all eight of the girls were around the table, smiling.

Nalala stood. "We all decided the house wasn't complete. Well, not yet. So yesterday when, you were milking Minerva…"

Childer whispered in Sam's ear, "You milked a Minerva?"

Sam poked Childer in the ribs with her elbow.

"… Well, Nachoka was taking pictures. Well, we all decided, that your mother and grandmother Lulu would want this."

Sam looked at them with a confused face. "Want what?"

In silence all eight of the girls looked up at the wall with the seven photographs. Sam realized there weren't seven photographs, but eight. A picture of her milking Minerva and smiling broadly had been added.

Childer wrapped his arm around Sam and whispered in her ear, "You look happy. You look really, *really* happy. Congratulations."

Sam's tears flowed freely. She went to each one of the girls, giving a long overdue hug.

When Sam returned to Childer, he burst out. "That's it! Sam! I've got it!"

Sam wiped the tears from her eyes with both hands. "Got what?"

"The name of your new company!"

▶◆◆◆◀

One year after Childer went to the ranch, he picked Sam up from San Francisco International Airport in a stretch limousine with a full bar.

"Why such opulence?" asked Sam.

"What? Can't I pick up an old friend in a city-style pickup truck?"

"Who's paying?" asked Sam as she eyed him warily.

"Don't worry about it. I'll charge it to your old firm," he laughed. "They still owe me anyway, cheap bastards."

"Well, I don't want you to get in trouble, but..." Sam smiled as she crawled into the car. "It would serve them right." She was no longer wearing Chanel but still looked fantastic in her $60.00 J. Crew dress. It wasn't that she didn't like the designer suits and dresses anymore. She just didn't feel it was 'her' any longer. But, her high heels, that was a different story. She wasn't about to give them up.

Thirty-five minutes later they were walking through the door of *Chapeau!,* a little French bistro rated one of the top ten best in San Francisco. There was a bottle of Dom Perignon sitting already chilled at their table. After being seated, the sommelier popped the cork and poured the flutes two-thirds full.

"Well, what shall we drink too?" asked Childer.

"I don't know. I'm still trying to figure out if the company is going to make it or not."

"Oh, let's not talk shop just yet," he smiled. "Let's enjoy the best San Francisco has to offer."

They clinked glasses and sipped the sparkling nectar as Sam looked around.

"This place is packed!"

"Mm…" Childer hummed, setting down his glass. "And it's *always* this way. I was here two weeks ago." He glanced at the table to his right, "There sat Zuckerberg with his entourage, and over there…" he nodded to a corner just behind Sam. "There sat Frankie Coppola."

"I thought Francis had his own place, down on Columbus?"

"He does, but this…" Childer poked the white linen covered table in rapid succession with his index finger. "This is the place everyone wants to be seen."

"Madame, sir, your menus," the waiter handed them the bill o' fare and took a step back. "If I may, the special is a petite fillet mignon in a trumpet mushroom and peppercorn sauce with broiled bone marrow and chervil. Our special appetizers are honey glazed dates with sprinkled blue cheese, and a fruit, nut, and cheese plate with passion fruit, honeyed pecans, gouda, cheddar, and brie."

Childer quickly glanced at the menu and asked the waiter, "What do you think of the cheese on the special, any good?"

Sam shot Childer a dirty look. Before she could lodge her protest, the waiter said, "Oh it's fanTASTIC! We just added it to the menu last week, and if I *do* say so myself, it's one of the *best things* we have on the list."

"That's mighty high praise!" said Childer with wide eyes. "What makes it so good?"

"In a word, it's the flavors. The cheeses are bright, lush, and well, opulent. It's vibrant and alive. It's, well… you try it," he smiled.

Childer smiled first at the waiter and then at Sam. "By any chance, do you know who makes the cheese and yogurt for the restaurant?"

"Oh, my yes! Hang on just a minute. Let me get something for you…" The waiter all but dashed behind the bar and came back with a glossy brochure, then handed it to Childer.

Sam glanced down at the brochure and froze.

"It's a little organic, cute as a button, mom-and-pop company out of New Mexico called *Eight Maids A Milking!* It's brilliant, isn't it?" the waiter asked, with a smile, then glanced at Sam, "Have you ever heard of them?"

She smiled. "Oh yes, I've heard of them," and looked at Childer. "I think that will be *just* fine."

IX

NINE LADIES DANCING

Nine Ladies Dancing

"Welcome back Ms. Jenkins," said a smiling orderly with Amos emblazoned over his left pocket.

Maud Jenkins, a lithe woman of fifty, walked through the Staff Only entrance at Walter Reed National Military Medical Center in Bethesda, Maryland, with her hair pulled back in a tight salt and pepper bun. She went directly to the Rehabilitation Center.

"Morning Amos. How is all today?"

"Oh, you know how it is. It's the same as before you left." He gave her a quick look of concern. "Does that husband of yours know you're back on duty?"

Maud sighed and shook her head, "No. I'd better go fight that dragon now." She turned and went to the elevator and pushed the button that said, "Administration Level."

She came out of the elevator like a woman on a mission, marching through the office door with *General Harold Jenkins M.D* on the nameplate.

"Harold, we need to talk."

Harold, sitting at a large, military issue desk, smiled, looking up at his cantankerous wife, "Maud? What can I do for you, my dear?"

"You can stop treating me with kid gloves."

"What? But I'm…"

"Oh, knock it off, Harold! I'm bored. You had me close my dance studio. You insisted I give up my job here. And if I don't die from this damn aneurism I'll die of boredom. So," she poked his desk with her index finger. "I've decided, I'm going back to work."

"Come again?"

"I didn't stutter. I'm going back to work."

"When? We go up to Rehoboth Beach for Labor Day next week."

"A half hour ago. I already moved all my equipment back into Rehab yesterday. As for the beach, we can go after the close of the season. It'll still be there." She leaned down and kissed him on the top of his bald spot before turning and marching out of the room. She didn't give him any options or time for a single word. He may have been the General in charge of the hospital, but in their relationship, she was the Commander in Chief. And they were well-matched. He watched her leave with a slight smile on his lips.

Once back in Rehab, Maud pulled charts of the new round of patients she would be working with. They were the first all-woman recovery team ever to be deployed. The military brass was hoping for a PR victory and headlines to read, "Women only strike team rescues female prisoner." All was going well, until the convoy of four vehicles was hit by an RPG barrage. Over half were KIA. The lucky few survivors were sent first to Ramstein Airforce Base in Germany, then here, to Walter Reed for Rehabilitation.

Maud read the cover notes before digging into the files. They read:

- **Dominique Smithers**—Kansas City, KS—lost her right arm and two ribs.
- **Katrina DuBouf**—New Orleans, LA— lost both eyes and a part of her right ear.
- **Euniqua Jones**—Harlem, NY—lost her left leg and hand.
- **Pauline Strummer**—Berea, OH—extensive chest and neck injuries, losing breasts, vocal cords, and a large amount of the tissue around her trachea.
- **Fran Martinez**—Santa Fe, NM—lost all her fingers, toes, nose and portions of her eyelids after being trapped by the steering wheel in the fire.
- **Abby Davenport**—Roanoke, VA—lost both arms at the elbow and over fifty percent of her hearing from the second blast after being thrown from the vehicle.
- **Whitney Morrison**—Junction City, KS—lost both legs and right eye.

When Maud got to the last name, her heart skipped three beats and she felt her stomach tighten. She read the top sheet:

- **Helen Farquhar**—Washington, DC. (Rescued Prisoner) Abrasions and bruises. Also, in a catatonic state.

Then she had to sit in the chair by the door, near to tears as she remembered her Helen. Helen was the daughter Maud never had, and the thought of seeing her like this sent ice through Maud's veins. Helen had been more than Maud's prize student and surrogate daughter. Maud's mind immediately went to her and Helen's first meeting in her studio. Helen was seven and showed many signs of being mentally abused. She was quiet, tentative, and overly apologetic when she made the smallest misstep. Helen's mother also showed signs of mental and at time physical abuse. She'd never look Maud in the eye and was always cagey about any bruises she'd have on her face and wrists, or a broken lip.

By contrast, Helen's army colonel father was gregarious, very hot tempered, and had nothing but disdain for arts. He was humorless and could not stand satirical comedy, calling it, "for those with weak minds." Upon meeting Maud for the first time his only comment was, "I don't want her to become some prissy dancer. No. I need her to have poise so she can stare down her troops. I expect her to be the first female three star General. Am I clear?"

It took two years for Maud to teach Helen it was okay to make mistakes. By the fourth year, Helen had passed all her classmates in aptitude and ability—leaping higher, spinning faster, and holding positions longer. Helen had always been full of life, talkative, and a joy, and Maud knew she was going to set the world on fire.

Maud called in favors from seven major companies and schools to get Helen auditions. When offers came from all, Helen's birth mother began to shut down and wouldn't speak of her only daughter leaving her. So, Maud had become Helen's stability, advisor, and de facto *real* mother. When Helen chose the scholarship and contracted to the New York City Ballet, both she and Maud were overjoyed. Helen's father was dead set against her living in "New York... that city of sin, that Sodom and Gomorrah." Maud tried to reach out to Helen's parents several times, but there was never any response.

Helen worked her way quickly through the corps and small roles, ending up dancing principal prima roles with New York City Ballet. Her talent could not be denied. She danced around the world, making a splash in Kiev, Berlin, and Paris with headlines reading, "A NEW PAVLOVA, ULANOVA, AND MARKOVA ROLLED INTO ONE!" and "BEAUTY, GRACE AND ELEGANCE-THY NAME IS FARQUHAR!"

But everything that rises—falls.

While on tour in Buenos Aires, she received a call from her father. Her mother had taken his service revolver, put the barrel in her mouth, and pulled the trigger. Helen landed in DC thirty-six hours later. She quickly fell back under her father's control. 'Shock' was too simple a word for what the ballet world felt when Helen retired at the age of twenty-two and enlisted in her father's beloved Army. With hard work, determination, and a dancer's endurance, Helen made it through boot camp. Six months after being deployed, she was captured, interrogated, and tortured in a small battle that took place in some oasis in the middle of a desert, that nobody'd ever heard of. That is, until Helen and her all-female rescue team were blown up.

That afternoon, all eight women were assembled in the rehab dance studio: some on crutches with prosthetic limbs, others in wheelchairs. All were in army-issue sweatpants and t-shirts while Maud had her hair up in a tight bun and wore her trademark scrubs with dancers printed on them, and white tennis shoes.

"Well, ladies, I know you've been though the ringer in Tal Afar, and everyone is proud of what you did there. Now it's time to get you up and moving again. Think of me as your DI. No, that does not stand for *Drill* Instructor. That stands for *Dance* Instructor. I'll be teaching you balance in your feet, bodies, and arms. More importantly I'll be helping you find balance in your brain, focus, and hearts."

A cascade of "Nope!" "Ain't gonna happen!" and "No way!" followed her introduction.

Maud saw the apprehension on their faces and said, "Look, I'm a classically trained ballet dancer and teacher. You try my patience, and I know how to hurt you. If you go above and beyond, I'll reward you with what you all *really* want."

"What's that?" asked Fran.

"Self-respect," smiled Maud.

Seven of the women stared daggers at the diminutive woman in front of them. Helen was in a wheelchair to the right of the pack, staring forward, lost in her own world.

"All right soldiers, this is your first class in coordination. We're going to *relearn* how to stand, walk, move, and eventually dance. Got it?" asked Maud from the front of the room.

"Hey. Who's the oldster?" Dominique whispered to Whitney.

"She's the general's wife, and don't let her fool you," Whitney smiled. "When I was stationed at Ramstein we heard everything about her. She used to be some big-deal ballerina back in Europe. After the General married her, she taught at some high-end ballet schools. A few years back, she started a new program here in Rehab, to re-teach balance and movement. She retired a few months ago. Rumor mill says she has an aneurism ready to pop."

"Don't upset general's wife." Katrina nodded. "Brain might pop, we get blamed. Roger that."

Maud raised her index finger in the air. "Now, to me, your injury does *not* matter. You're more than what you lost," then she pointed to her forehead, "You're whole up here, and here," she pointed to her heart. "So, no, 'I can't do it's!'" She suddenly sounded like a drill instructor. "Do I make myself clear?"

"Yes ma'am!" came a full-throated reply.

"Good! Then let's start. Who of you has had any formal dance training?" Pauline Strummer and Helen were the only two who had formal training.

Maud knelt next to Helen's wheelchair, putting her fingers over Helen's cupped hand, trying to look into her eyes. The eyes were open wide, but not focusing. "Come on my dear girl, I know you're in there. I know they didn't take you away from me," Maud whispered.

▶◆◆◆◀

"You want me to *what*? No *way* can I gets my arms up there. Not like that," protested Dominique late in the fourth week of rehab. "And these big boats," she said, looking at her feet. "Ain't *never* stuck in those directions before. *Nope*, ain't gonna happen." She had her natural arm resting on top of her head while her prosthetic arm stuck straight up in the air. Her feet were side by side pointing straight forward.

Maud didn't skip a beat, holding her feet in fifth position—feet overlapping with the right in front of the left, and each foot pointing directly away from each other at 180 degrees. "Chicken, huh?"

Dominique scowled, "Chicken? I ain't chicken of *nothing*!"

"So, you say. Then, why *not* do what I'm doing? Good *Lord* woman! I'm easily three times your age!"

The room hushed watching the faceoff between Maud and Dominique. In one mighty grunt, Dominique lifted her crooked arm and the bent prosthetic into position—mirroring Maud—above her head and held them there for three seconds. Fatigue tremors started on her weak side and her arms came down, causing her to gasp.

"*WooHoo!*" "Awesome!" "Yeeeaaass!" came from the surrounding women.

Maud dropped the position and embraced Dominique with a broad smile. "See! I told you; you could do it! It was beautiful!

"You see ladies, you must be *thrifty* with all your movements. You can't flail about and hope your limbs end up where you want them. No. You must think, imagine, *then* move." Maud turned back to Dominique and said, "Now, I want you to do that position three or four more times today; we'll build on that."

Dominique smiled at the slight, elderly dancer and asked, "I'm gonna *what*? You're *crazy!*"

"I may be crazy," retorted Maud. "But you just did a move you *knew* you couldn't. So, who's *crazy* now, huh?" she said, mocking.

Dominique hung her head and a huge smile broke free. "You're gonna kill me yet, little miss."

Maud smiled and teased, "What doesn't kill you makes you stronger," then passed by Helen's wheelchair, but there was no recognition.

"Oh, my dear, dear girl…" Maud whispered, slightly shaking her head. "What have they done to you?" She bent and began to manipulate Helen's feet, calves, and legs. Stretching and pulling. After ten minutes of work on Helen's lower extremities Maud became dizzy and stood up quickly. "Well now…" she huffed. "I think I need to take a bit of a break." Maud held her hand to the left side of her head and heard pounding. "Well, *that's* new."

Maud made her way to a chair and sat hard, head in her hands. The women stopped what they were doing and looked in her direction. Feeling the eyes on her, Maud looked up and said, "It's nothing, just a bit of fatigue. I'm fine. Now Whitney, see if you can balance your wheelchair on just two wheels, sort of like a bicycle popping a wheely."

No one seemed to notice, but even though Helen was staring forward, her feet and legs were lifting and twitching while still in the chair.

A week later was what Maud called, "Show and Tell." Charlie Collins, the pianist Maud had used in her private studio for over thirty years, came to play for the now mid-rehab dancer's first private recital. All eight women were dressed in their sweats and t-shirts, ready to show what they could do.

"All right ladies, I want to see your progress. I've given you the music you'll be dancing to. But I've left the choreography of your routines to you." she clapped. "Let's see what you've accomplished. Katrina and Whitney, you're first up." She looked to the piano, "Charlie?"

The slight white-haired accompanist snapped his head up to Maud's call. "Yes, ma'am?"

"Tchaikovsky, *Sugar Plum Fairy,* if you please."

"Yes, ma'am."

As the music started, Katrina DeBouf (bandages still over her eyes) pushed Whitney Morrison's wheelchair to the center of the room, Whitney posed her arms and torso in beautiful forms, like a dancer gliding across ice, as Katrina rounded to the front of the wheelchair. Without warning, she lifted Whitney over her left shoulder and began spinning, Whitney silently and secretly tapping on Katrina's shoulders, telegraphing where the front of the room was located. As the final strains of the high tinkling wound to a halt, Katrina laid Whitney back into the wheelchair with gentle finesse. Then Whitney popped a wheely, and Katrina lithely lay beneath the front of the chair in a slight fetal position, looking almost like a sleeping child.

After five seconds of total silence, the room exploded into applause and whoops, tears flowing freely.

"That was freaking amazing!"

"No way?"

"Awesome!"

"Now *that*," Maud approached waving her finger at the couple. "...was the most amazing example of ballet I've ever seen. Well done. Well done, indeed!" She hugged Katrina and Whitney close as tears came. They had done it. The unthinkable. They were becoming whole again.

▶◆◆◆◀

Two weeks after the first "Show and Tell" Maud strode into the room of waiting women. All were sitting at the far end of the dance studio/rehab room and waited to hear in what order they would be dancing.

"Ladies, I have an announcement. I am coming to you after a meeting with my husband and the Vice President of the United States. We will be producing a dance review for Christmas at the White House."

The room sat in stunned silence.

"No, I'm not kidding, and no, I'm not going to cut you any slack. I just committed you as the entertainment for the Christmas gathering and dinner for the President and First Lady on December 23. I told you I'd push you to your limits. Now," she pointed and looked at the calendar on the far wall. "This gives you exactly forty-five days to turn yourselves into professional dancers. Got it?"

Still no expression from anyone in the room.

"Good. No backtalk, that's what I like to hear. Now, let's get to it." Maud strode over to her waiting chair and table

next to Charlie and his piano. Sitting next to her was Helen,
who was now walking under her own power, but only if she
were led. She was still in her own world. Maud was hoping
She'd waken and come back to the world that was her life
blood—music and dance.

"No, no, no... You need to raise your arms like *this*!
What you're doing looks like a wounded turkey. And we all
know what happens to wounded turkeys this time of year."
Maud shook her perfectly manicured index finger in the face
of Pauline Strummer, chiding her.

Maud, leaned into Helen and whispered, "Look at them
my dear. Just look at them. None of them have the talent you
had. No, *have*," she corrected herself. "They work *so* hard
and don't give up. They don't stop. They just keep pushing,
and pushing, and pushing..." she trailed off in admiration.
"They're like—like the Valküre! Strong women, sent by Odin
himself to ferry warrior's souls to Walhalla." She looked at
Helen, "Do you remember the Valküre routine I gave you to
dance when you were fifteen or sixteen?" Maud looked back
at the women. The idea that she was now working with real
flesh and blood Valküre made her warm inside.

"You know," Maud looked over at Helen. "I'm giving
them that same routine you used to dance in my studio, before you went to the New York Ballet." Maud frowned and
looked at the floor. "Of course, there will be modifications.
Nobody can dance that piece like you can." Maud looked

away. She realized she'd momentarily forgotten that this wasn't the "old" Helen.

Maud stopped and looked at Helen's vacant eyes. For a split second, she thought she saw a glimmer of recognition. "Oh, my dear girl, what I wouldn't give to see you dance the solo at the end one more time." Maud hung her head as the tears quietly rolled down her cheeks.

►◆◆◆◄

"Thrifty my ass!" yelled Maud into the telephone's receiver.

There was a voice on the other end making excuses and a very sterile, "I'm sorry" was heard, but Maud was having none of it.

"All right, you tell me what we're supposed to do. The girls have been measured for their costumes; we've sent the music list to the Army Band for the dances." Maud felt a dizzy spell coming and sat down in the folding chair. "We're going to the White House… The *White House* for cripe sake! We can't perform in front of the President in old grubby fatigues and using cell phones for music! It's just not right!"

The voice at the other end made a few more apologies but was not budging.

After Maud slammed down the receiver, she went into the Rehab room. "All right, gather around," Maud breathed deeply. "I have some news."

"Uh-Oh. We're still going to the White House, ain't we?" asked Dominique.

"Yes dear," smiled Maud. "Why do you ask?"

Because, nobody says, 'I have some news' like you just did if its *good* news."

"Well, you're partially right, we are still going to the White House, but we won't have any costumes. Or…" she felt a bit dizzy, but continued, "or an orchestra."

Pauline picked up her white board, and began to scrawl quickly, "Don't need costumes or orchestra. Improvise." She turned it around for all to see.

"Hell, yeah!"

"That's what I'm talking about!"

"Boo Yah!" were the replies.

"All right ladies," smiled Maud. "What are your ideas? We need to tell a story."

"Well," said Fran, "We are soldiers, and we are like those women who fly outta the sky for Odin. Why don't we tell that story in our own way?"

"Right," added Euniqua. "Why don't we just do it in fatigues? We *know* how to move in those."

"Damn straight," and "Hell yeah!" echoed in the room.

"Now," Maud broke in, "tradition says there were eight Valküre shuttling souls." She looked at Helen, now standing to her right clutching her hands to her chest and staring straight forward. "But you are only seven at this point, so I will dance the eighth with you."

"No, no, no…" rattled off Dominique. "You can't do that, there's something wrong in your head!"

"I assure you," said Maud casually. "There's nothing wrong with my head."

"Yes, there is… You've got an angina or something up there. That's what they said when we asked about those dizzy spells of yours," said Euniqua.

"We asked your husband," said Katrina, meekly.

"Well," said Maud looking from face to concerned face. "I've been dancing this same finale on stage since before you were born. I assure you; it's not taxing, and I'll modify it down. Now," Maud said, quickly changing the subject. "What props will we need? What story do we want to tell? You're not too thrilled with Tchaikovsky, what different music do we want to use?"

▶◆◆◆◀

As Maud and her dancers pulled up to the White House gate on December twenty-third, Maud felt as if her head and body weren't attached to the ground. Normally she'd tell someone, but today, God himself wasn't getting in the way of her Valküre performing for the President of the United States, the Cabinet, and honored guests. The women entered the East Room of the White House with wide eyes and gaping mouths. They'd never seen anything so opulent. The iconic room was now decorated with festive Christmas balls from the ceiling and real pine branches and tinsel swags lining the walls.

"Ms. Maud! We're dancing up *there*?" asked Dominique pointing to the stage dominating the entire north side of the East room. Maud nodded her head, while still feeling dizzy and detached. She turned to her troops, and said, "All right ladies, get up on stage!"

As the rehearsal progressed, Maud worked with the girls and finally got them to focus, becoming more comfortable in their surroundings. Maud pulled her old pair of pastel pink toe shoes out of a worn canvas bag and tied them on. She looked around but couldn't find Helen, she had slipped away. In the past month Helen had progressed to the point where she was mobile, getting physically stronger, and self-determined again. But there still were no signs of her listening to anyone in her surroundings. Maud went down the steps of the platform and found Helen, doing dancers deep knee bends in front of a mirror that had been brought in for the event. Maud's heart surged. Helen had strengthened physically, but still was in her own world; seemingly not making contact with anyone around her.

"Helen, my dear," asked Maud with a smile. "How are you feeling?"

No answer.

Maud heard the warm-up music beginning to wind down and knew she would have to dance soon. She took Helen's hand and squeezed it tightly. "Come back to me my dear. Come back." She turned her head toward the stage and said, "All right, time to rehearse."

Maud wasn't tentative at all. When her cue music came, she burst out from behind the first leg from off offstage and did a grand jetè, then stately arabesque. She was a bit slower and didn't have the airtime she once had, but for the next seven and a half minutes, she moved with skill and determination.

At nine minutes, she made a grand sweep around the stage alternating between grand jetès and pirouettes. As she moved on from point to point, one of the Valküre would stand in the spot she had just left, making a grand arc of wounded women warriors.

Once back in center, she began a spinning arabesque that had everyone in the room glued to her motion. Maud didn't want the dancing to end. It had been too long since she'd been allowed to feel invigorated by the dance floor under her feet and her body responding to the music. When she stopped, she called down to the accompanist, "Hey, Charlie!"

"Yes?"

"How long has it been since we just, played?"

Charlie began to grin, "Too long!"

Charlie and Maud—two consummate artists—began to play together, doing a form of improvisation they had done in the studio many times. Charlie would play snippets of what he'd played before and watch for cues from Maud as to when to change to a new piece. Charlie played samples of all seven pieces from the women's dances, and Maud enacting the Valküre's routines until she signaled for the end.

The twenty or so guards, workman, waiters, and technicians burst into applause. The eight dancers were all smiles, some had tears, others giggled into their hands. Charlie began to play prearranged music for the curtain call and the other eight ladies took one long, graceful, and deserved bow.

Maud came to the backstage right area and reached for a towel that was tossed over her toe shoe bag. She noticed Helen sitting in the chair next to her bag, holding and staring at a second pair of toe shoes Maud had packed.

"My dear girl, I wish you were out there tonight. I've never danced with true heroes before. And, I expect, I never will again."

After the dinner had ended and the First Family and dignitaries had been seated in the audience, Maud gathered her Valküre around her for final instructions.

"Know I am prouder of you than I've ever been. Your beauty, determination, and sheer willpower has turned each of you into a swan."

Abby elbowed Fran and asked, "She just call us swamps?"

Everyone chuckled and Maud turned, looking directly at Abby. "No, my dear. I called you swans." Maud shaped her hand and arm into a swan's head and neck. "Swan dear... not swamp."

"Oh..." said Abby laughing with recognition and all the women chuckling along with her.

"All right ladies, take your places, concentrate, and for God's sake... have fun!"

Charlie looked back to Maud, and she nodded to him to begin to play the opening music to the dance set.

The first two to dance were Whitney and Katrina, in a slight revision of their first dance in the Rehab room. Instead of Tchaikovsky, Charlie played Wagner's 'Ride of the Walküre'. The motion of the music added to the gliding of Whitney's wheelchair. Without warning, the music became percussive, driving, stately. Katrina pantomimed being shot, then lay on the ground, wounded in battle, writhing briefly, eventually succumbing to her wounds. Whitney's Valküre swooped and spun, emulating with her wheelchair the movements of the steed of a Valküre. As she beckoned to the spirit of the fallen soldier, Katrina came to life, moving in a mix of ballet and modern dance. To ensure Katrina's blindness would not be a factor, small playing cards were mounted to the wheels of the wheelchair, much like an eight-year-olds bicycle, giving her Whitney's placement on stage.

As Katrina nestled into the wheelchair atop Whitney, Abby and Euniqua came out in tandem, wearing an apparatus allowing them to meld into one body—Abby walked and danced, Euniqua moved her arms and torso. In dim light, the two merged into one body and soon all front light was gone, leaving them in silhouette with bright lights shining through a white China silk backdrop. The two were in a harness back-to-back, so when they turned profile, the view was quite shocking as it almost looked like an ancient Indian God with extra arms, prosthetics, and heads. As the music— Charlie played Gustav Holtz's, 'Mars' from *The Planets*— swelled, Euniqua would grab different cutouts of weapons from history, thrusting and slashing them against the evil figments projected onto the China silk, like an Indonisian puppet show. When the creatures seemed to be getting the best of Abby/Euniqua, they would begin to do handsprings, rotating into somersaults; the ground being caught by Euniqua's strong arms would be pushed off on to Abby's stable feet.

The two cartwheeled off to stage left, allowing Pauline, dressed in white tie and black tuxedo with tails, to escort Fran, dressed in a flowing champagne pink ball gown, onto the dance floor. They gracefully danced waltzes and foxtrots, to a medley of Andrew's Sisters tunes, sung by a trio lent to the event from the local opera company.

While Pauline and Fran were starting the foxtrot, Maud sat down next to Helen, almost missing the chair. Her toe shoes dangling from her left hand while her right hand was up over her eyes and forehead.

"Oh my..." she breathed in a high-pitched voice. "I don't... I don't know what's wrong with... with me." Maud couldn't focus her eyes and turned to Helen in momentary blindness.

"Helen, my sweet Helen. I'm not sure I can do this."

Maud felt Helen's right hand touching her shoulder.

"Helen? Helen dear…" she asked blindly. "Can you hear me? Are you with me?"

Helen didn't answer, nor did she look to her second mother. She continued to stare at the floor. But her hand was grasping Maud's shoulder.

"My dear girl, I…" Maud leaned forward in her chair, turning slightly, but never made it. Maud slid off the chair, onto the floor, and lay there, looking up at Helen, sight momentarily returning. Staring up into her eyes. Maud saw something. It was more than a spark, it was recognition.

"Helen… My dear Helen." The toe shoes fell to the floor and Maud's hand began to spasm uncontrollably. "I… You! You need to… You need to dance… for me! Dance for mm…"

Helen didn't seem to notice as the stage manager came back and saw Maud's entire body racked in spasms. A medic from Walter Reed was found and Maud was quietly put on a stretcher and taken to the hospital. Maud's husband, General Jenkins, was standing next to Helen as he was informed his wife was being transported back to Walter Reed by ambulance. Through it all, Helen looked forward, to the stage, to the dancing, as tears began to slowly course down her face.

As Pauline and Fran's routine ended, Dominique and Euniqua entered the stage with an eight-foot length of rope between them. Charlie at this point had received word that Maud had been taken to the hospital. Fighting back tears, he planned how to end, the now pounding Stravinsky's "Firebird". The two danced with fury and flight, becoming one with the rope and the soaring music.

The other six dancers looked on as Dominique and Euniqua continued their almost primal dance. Everyone expected to see Maud in the wings, watching her Walküre dance.

Instead, Abby pointed out a pair of petal pink toe shoes lying on the floor next to Helen's wheelchair. By the time Pauline had retrieved her white board and scrawled, "Where?" the toe shoes had vanished. All six performers were across stage, where they could see Helen but kept moving up and down stage to catch sight of Maud.

In the last eight bars of "the Firebird," Charlie heard the distinct setting of tempo by a pair of tapping toe shoes. He smiled broadly in relief, knowing the information about Maud and her condition had been wrong. She would be dancing on stage in under four bars.

Charley pounded the final cadence of "the Firebird" as the lights quickly softened for the petal pink toe shoes and olive-green explosion about to emanate from stage right.

On cue there was a burst from the wings as Charlie thrust his hands into the keys. The opening chord of Grieg's 'A' Minor Piano Concerto' was followed by an almost deafening gasp, first from her fellow dancers, then from the audience who had heard Helen's story. There, on stage, wearing fatigues and pink toe shoes was Helen Farquhar, ex-prisoner of war, daughter of an army Colonel, and ex-ballerina. On this night, the "ex" would be removed.

Helen fell into the very familiar dance routine like the professional she was. She'd been dancing a variation of this dance for many years and knew it better than the color of her best friend's eyes. She'd became a real dancer with *this* routine many years before and was revisiting her old friend.

The astounded audience began to whisper and titter about Helen's virtuosity. Her arabesque was the perfect definition of angular beauty. Her grand jetè sent her sailing, almost as if she were a marionette with invisible wires. Her piqué work astounded everyone. The toes of her shoes looked like little darts barely puncturing the stage, a hummingbird stabbing a peach for its nectar.

The women who saved her life came out one by one, all crying silent tears, taking their positions on stage. They had never seen anything so beautiful; they had never seen a comrade in arms burst forth, like a true Phoenix.

Helen came to the center of the stage and finished the routine with grace, poise, and beauty. As her mentor had before her, she looked down and caught Charlie's eye. Charlie gave a nodded, smile intact, tears liberally falling on his keys.

Just as with Maud, Charlie began to improvise from all the pieces of the evening, weaving them together seamlessly.

This was something usually not done in pre-programmed dance, but Maud and Charlie had begun doing with their students to get them to think on their feet. As long as the dancers danced, Charlie would weave the music under them. It was symbiotic, unplanned, thrilling.

The dance continued for five, seven, then nine minutes in a sonorous tornado of notes, dancers, and emotion. Helen wove between each of her saviors in tableau on stage, giving each a personal acknowledgment and wordless, "Thank you. Thank you for being here. Thank you for rescuing me. Thank you for helping me come out of the dark shell I've been in since saving my life." Feeling the familiar fatigue settling into her bones, Helen decided it was time to stop dancing, and become human again.

As a signal to Charlie that it was time to end, Helen stepped to the front center portion of the stage and began to pirouette, spinning faster, and faster, allowing her arms to undulate in, out, up, and down. Each and every movement created a different picture, a different form, evoking a different emotion. When her flight ended, she stopped in a final pose. A pin dropping on the carpet would have sounded like a grenade. The East Room of the White House was stone silent for five full seconds. The room exploded into applause and resounding calls of "Bravo!" that continued for a full ten minutes. They had witnessed miracles.

After the standing ovation, and a speech recognizing them for their hard work, the President asked Maud to come to the stage, he wanted to give her a special gift. In heavy silence the stage manager approached the leader of the free world and whispered in his ear. Obviously shaken, he cleared his throat and turned to the women who were still smiling.

"You eight women are a true inspiration. Facing the adversity. Using your dexterity. Showing the mental and physical fortitude... They are unmatched." The President looked away and cleared his throat while looking at the floor. "I do have some news about your leader, Ms. Maud Jenkins. Ms. Jenkins was taken to Walter Reed." The president now turned fully to the women before him. "I regret to tell you; she passed tonight on the way to the hospital. I am very sorry for your loss."

Shock moved like a wave throughout the room. As the information became understood in the audience, the eight women clung to each other for support.

Helen stepped away from the group and came to the President, who silently relinquished the microphone. The seven dancers stared at Helen in disbelief. She was now fully back. When they found her, she was barely alive, barely breathing, barely—human.

"Tonight, no words can carry weight. No glance can tell the full story. Tonight, lives were changed." Helen had tears streaming freely as she spoke. "Beginning with mine. Maud was more than a teacher and dancer; she was my second mother. She believed in me when all, including myself, gave up hope. I can..." Helen looked to the other women on stage, "*we* can all say we lost *our* mother. And that there were not eight, but *nine* ladies dancing up here tonight. She made us whole. She gave us a second chance to be alive. She made us who we are today."

Helen stepped away from the mic and went to her fellow Valküre, hugging them close. Helen looked at them and said, "To the nine ladies dancing tonight," she then looked upward, toward heaven. "We love you, mama Maud."

TEN LORDS A LEAPING

Ten Lords a Leaping

"Hey old-timer, what are ya havin'?" asked a buff, dark-haired man in his forties dressed in a cotton and fire-retardant red jumpsuit. He smelled like smoke and had "Harry" and Hot Shot" embroidered on a Velcro patch over his left breast pocket. "Let me buy you another round."

The older man sat on the stool at the back corner of the bar, wearing an old, tattered army-issue rain jacket with holes burnt into it, and an old cap with "Smoke Jumper" embroidered on the front. He looked up at the much younger man, lifted his empty glass, and said, "Bushmills, double, neat."

"Woah now, that's a real man's drink. You sure your meds will react okay with that?" joked Harry.

The older man looked up to his left at an aged picture on the wall. "Screw the drugs. Don't care. I need to salute my nine."

The door of Smokey's Bar and Grill opened, and eight men and women poured in, all dressed in standard-issue red jump suits with yellow slickers and name patches.

"Hey Harry! What are ya havin'? chuckled a soot-covered woman with short, sweat-soaked blonde hair and Betty on her name badge.

"I'll have what the old-timer's having, double Bushmills." He smiled over his shoulder at the older man. "No ice."

The ragtag group came to where their leader stood, next to the old man on the bar stool.

'Who's the oldster?" asked a short, stout firefighter, wiping the grime off of his face with a dish towel from behind the bar.

The elder man looked up with basset hound eyes. "George. George Pulaski."

The bartender dropped off George's and Harry's double Bushmills then took the group's orders.

"Whoa, Pulaski, like the fire ax, Pulaski?" asked Betty.

George shifted his eyes to her. "Ed Pulaski was my father." He designed that ax so he could fight fires better. It's been around a long time." He looked back at the bar, "Like me."

He picked up the Bushmills and raised it to Harry in salute, then to the picture behind him and put the glass to his mouth. In one motion, he poured the drink down. Not flinching, not grimacing, George put the glass back on the bar and stared at it.

The move caught everyone's attention. A Hot Shot with Brad on his chest muttered, "Damn! That takes balls."

George continued to look forward and said, "That ain't nothin'." He pointed an arthritic finger to the picture. "You should have seen the balls on those boys."

Harry kept the glass to his lips and swallowed twice, having to put the glass down and wince at the strong burn. He put his left hand on George's shoulder and asked, "Who were they? They look like they're up in the higher Sierras."

George picked up his glass and lifted it toward the bartender without a word while looking back at the picture. "We were known as the 'Lord's Leapers.' Doubt if you've ever heard of us."

Harry lifted his glass back to his lips. "No, can't say I have."

The bartender brought the fresh drink to George and took the empty glass from him.

"We ten were the first paratrooper firefighters in the United States. We drink a glass for each one of the boys who've passed. We started a tradition after we lost Willie and Bernie. We'd drink a double to each man." George nodded to the bartender after she filled his glass.

"Wait a minute," asked the short stocky firefighter. "How old are you in that picture?"

They crowded around George, taking a better look at the picture.

"We were all twenty-one to twenty-three." George lifted his left index finger and pointed to the third man from the left. "I was the youngest of the Lords." ·

"How did you get your name? I mean, '*Lord's Leapers*' isn't a normal moniker," asked one of the fighters with a burn scar on left side of his neck and Juan on his jacket.

"Oh, that story will take another drink..." Harry lifted his finger, and another Bushmills was sat in front of him.

►♦♦♦◄

March, 1945

"Hey Jimmy, what are you going to do after we're sent back stateside?" asked the slight but muscular soldier, giving his parachute one last check on the British Airforce DC3 approaching its target near Berlin, Germany.

"Aw, I expect I'll head home to Truckee and do some fishing around Lake Tahoe. What about you Harold? What are you going to do?"

A very muscular man in uniform tipped his helmet back, "I guess me, and my brother, will go back to the family farm. Expect our Ma and Pa need the help." He turned to his right. "What about you, Lieutenant? Are you staying in merry old England, or are you going to come with us Yanks and try a new life in the US?"

The man at the front of the plane wearing a British Lieutenant's uniform took two steps closer to the eleven men in front of him and replied in a perfectly proper British accent, "I am a Lord. You Yanks wouldn't recognize my station, and I would have to leave my family estates. No, I do believe I'll be headed back to London and Parliament. But…"

The green 'go' light began to flash and all twelve men moved to the now, open door of the plane.

►◆◆◆◄

"We lost Lieutenant Lord Chauncey Beauchamp on that drop. And we lost Barry Greiner, a good old boy from Texas, I think he said his Pa was a wildcatter. One was shot on the way down, the other got hung up in a tree. Snapped his neck on impact.

"After the war, the ten of us that were left shipped home and took up our lives. It didn't take long before all of us felt bored, unneeded, and out of place, like the world moved on without us. After six months, we all decided to meet up somewhere. None of us had been to Lake Tahoe before, except Jimmy Gallagher, and he lived there. So, we decided to meet up August 1, that was in 1946.

"Ouch!" said a stocky firefighter named Steve. "That was the year they had fire tornadoes up in the El Dorado."

George looked over his shoulder at the man. "That's right. I'm surprised anyone's ever heard about that."

"I heard all about it from my grandpa. He lost an entire herd of sheep and goats to the fire. He said the flames slithered and shot up the mountainside in about ten minutes. He barely had enough time to save my grandma and one good herding dog."

"That's right. It was a hot one," smiled George, taking another sip from his glass. "We all went to Jimmy's, over in Truckee, but couldn't find him. Instead, he left a note saying, 'Sorry boys, I'm fighting a fire down in Colfax. Come on down if you want to have some fun!"

"Well sir, we just looked at each other and smiled. We all loaded into a couple of old broken-down trucks and the nine of us headed down the hill. It took us no more than about thirty minutes to find Jimmy. He was wearing his old jump helmet and a slicker holding one of my Pa's axes.

▶◆◆◆◀

August 1946

"I knew you boys couldn't stay away."

"Hell Jimmy, we couldn't let you have all the fun!" said a redhaired, stringy, ex-soldier."

"Aw Bob, you have no idea how much fun this really is! It's hot, noisy, dangerous... and you get that kick... It's just plain fun," Jimmy laughed.

"Well? Where do we sign up?" asked the blonde-haired blue-eyed man with 'Larry,' embroidered on the left side of his work shirt.

Jimmy tossed his head over his left shoulder. "Talk to that tall drink of water over there. He's the fight boss..."

►◆◆◆◄

"In about fifteen minutes, we were all suited up with axes, water sprayers, and rakes to go back into battle. Our first charge was a slope about twenty miles up into the Sierras. There were flames shooting a hundred foot high, and the embers were swirling like an orange blizzard. Now mind you, we had no training in fighting fires. Hell, the only thing we ever fought before that was the Nazi bastards. But we did know how to forest fight.

"We set an attack line about eight or ten feet apart and started raking, and chopping, and spraying as we went. It didn't take us an hour to realize we were losing the battle. We were only putting the fire out right in front of us and weren't doing a damn thing about its advance. We were constantly in the rears.

"Willie Brunelleschi," George pointed to the farthest man to the right in the photo. "He was the wiseacre of the ten of us. He called all of us together late that night and said, 'Ya know, I do believe I know how the Krauts felt. We ain't making no headway.' He stood up tall and looked to his left, then right, then came back down with the rest of us and said, 'Don't know about the rest of ya, but I'm midnight requisitioning a chainsaw and takin' a little hike around the flank. I'm gonna see if I can fight Satan head-on.'

"It didn't take us long to grab ten chainsaws and fuel that weren't ours, and get to the downwind side of the fire. Once there, we backed up about a quarter mile and began digging and chopping. We figured if there wasn't anything to burn, the fire would put itself out. Hell, we were making it up as we went. Sure enough, by the time the fire caught up with us we were dead dog tired, but we all picked up our spray cans and began pumping and spraying to beat the band. We actually whipped it!"

"That must've been close to the first time anyone had trenched a fire. I don't think that became standard practice for another five or ten years," said Harry.

"Yup," said George, taking a sip of water from a glass that was in front of him. "That was the first we'd heard of it. The fight boss came up to us the next day and wanted to know if we all wanted a full-time job, there were more and more fires devastating the Sierras every year. Before the war, it didn't matter much. There weren't that many people living up in the woods. But now, well, everyone wanted to get away. He said we'd get flown or driven to wherever the hotspots were in California."

"That means you were part of the first team of full-time forest firefighters in California!" said Betty.

"Hell Missy, we were the first full-time forest firefighters in the US. And we had a good time doing it. None of us were attached, no girlfriends, wives, or whatever... and to be honest, none of us had an inkling to get hitched. See, war did a little number on our brains. Too much death and destruction. We all needed a good shot of adrenaline to make us sleep through the night in peace. Well, not peace. I don't think any of us ever found any peace."

"So how long did you all work the fires?" asked Juan.

George looked back at him and nodded, seeing the telltale rippled skin of a burn victim on his neck. "Looks like you know what it's like to get kissed by the flame. Well, we outflanked all the rest of the fires that year. If memory serves me, that would've been fifteen; none bigger than say eighty acres. For the most part, we were badger rats."

"Badger rats?" asked Steve.

"That's what they used to call trench diggers back in the day," said Harry.

"Kudos for knowing your history!" agreed George, setting down his glass. "We dug trenches all the rest of that year and half of the next. Then, we had a big storm in the back country, up around Redding. Well sir, it would've taken us a day and a half to even get to the base of the fire, let alone on the leeward side. We had everybody trying to figure out how to cut in a road or trail, so we could get to the front side of the blaze. It took two days and about three hundred acres before Willie said, 'What the hell is wrong with you lemmings? Didn't we fly and take a leap for Lieutenant Lord Chauncey Beauchamp himself? Why the hell don't we just take a plane up, jump out, drop in behind the enemy line, and fight this Hell Demon the way we know how?'

"Well sir, no one in our upper command had ever heard of such a thing, and they didn't want to take a risk with ten firefighters' lives."

"Because you were too valuable," said Steve.

"No," smirked George. "No, because they thought they'd have to pay us more. They didn't realize we didn't care about the pay. We cared about the job. It was all we knew, fighting and honor. Hell, without that, we all knew we'd shrivel up and die.

"So, that night, as the bigwigs were still jawing about what to do, the ten of us got our pilot a bit tipsy. Not so drunk he couldn't fly, mind you, but greased enough he'd do what we asked him to. After about three hours of drinking, we drove him out to the tarmac, then cranked up the engines on the DC3.

"The flight only took a half hour. By sun-up, we were dancing with the devil." George took a long look at the picture, then reached for his glass and finished his fifth tribute. He looked up at the bartender, holding his glass up.

"Whoa now George, don't you think you've had enough?" cautioned Harry.

George shot Harry a look of, "You ain't my mamma," at Harry, then waved the glass at the bartender who filled it and stepped away.

"That fire took us two-and-a-half weeks to kill off. The one thing we learned from that dance was we needed more equipment, someplace to sleep, and good maps."

"Wait, you didn't have a map of the area?" asked Betty, ordering another drink.

"No ma'am." George drank the top off of the glass of whiskey. "That first time jumping in behind the line, we did half-assed. We didn't know the terrain, we didn't know how far we were from the closest water source, hell we didn't even know where the nearest town was. We were totally blind."

"So, what happened?" asked Harry.

"Well, come every twelve hours, round 8 AM and 8 PM, half of us would hike a half-mile windward. We'd dig a small trench about two feet deep and line it with moss. After, we'd clear trees for a hundred feet around, then hunt for berries and water and lay all we found in the trench. Like I said, we didn't think ahead."

"Why the trench?" asked the man Juan."

"So, the other crew would have somewhere a little safer to catch three- or four-hours sleep and not have to look for food and water. While they were getting shut eye, the rest would be battling. The next day, we'd reverse it, and the other team would trench, clear and scavenge while we slept. It's what we knew how to do. That's what we did in 'The Fatherland,' when we were over there. One war is like another, just different enemies. Only with a fire there's no Armistice. There's no truce, no half measures. You either kill it, or be killed." George looked at the faces around him. "Aw hell, I'm just preachin' to the choir. You know what I'm sayin'."

"That's amazing!" blurted out Brad, now sitting at the bar. "How is it I've never heard of any of this before?"

George took a deep drink on the glass in front of him and set it down very carefully. "Because of what happened around seven years later."

"What?" asked Harry.

"By that time, we'd battled over a hundred fires and made at least fifty jumps. By then it was the 1950s and a Senator by the name of McCarthy was pointing fingers at so-called communists."

"I don't get it, what's that got to do with fire jumping?" asked Harry.

"Absolutely nothing," said George, lifting his glass for a fill up. "See, the boys back in DC had heard about the ten of us leaping out of planes and fighting fires. Somebody at the Pentagon got their knickers in a twist saying we were battle-hardened soldiers from World War II, obviously preparing for the next war."

"But that doesn't make sense. You were all of thirty-plus years old by that point, right?" asked Betty.

"A gold star for the mathematician!" chuckled George. "No, some jar head or bean counter at the Pentagon convinced McCarthy that we were communist sympathizers, practicing our paratrooping skills and teaching them to another generation, just so we could sympathize with the Reds that were going to attack at any given moment."

"That's insane!" yelped Juan.

George looked over at him. "Insane or not, that's what the bastards did. We were doing great work. Groundbreaking work. Work that was saving lives. But politics got in the way and almost shut us down. We had to make all of our jumps at night for the next four or five years. The politicians didn't want to chance anyone seeing parachutes dropping down, even though it was obvious we were there to fight the fire."

George lifted his glass to the picture over his shoulder and took another drink, finishing off his eighth glass. "By 1962, all ten of us had burn scars, inhalation issues, and spent well over a month in the hospital at some point. Then it happened." He got a faraway look and stared at the picture on the wall for a good minute.

"You okay, George?" asked Harry softly.

George looked back at the bar, nodding, and taking a slow drink; a single tear dropping from his right eye. "We made the jump that night; hell, we'd done over thousand like it over our lifetimes. But this time there was a gust of wind that came out of nowhere. We'd leapt outta the plane about a quarter mile away from where the fire line was. We thought we were far enough away. For that matter, Jimmy thought we were too far out.

"First Willie," George pointed up to a man in the picture, then shifted to another. "Then Bernie began to drift. The up-draft from the fire met the wind coming in from the east. They started spinning like they were caught in a whirlpool.

Both of their parachutes collapsed and ended up dropping straight down — *Blam!*" George slapped both of his hands hard on the oak bar. "Well sir, we found their charred remains the next day. Not much left but ashes and dog tags.

"After that, the eight of us would make jumps a little farther away from the line; and the brass started making us train new kids. But it wasn't the same. Them kids couldn't read our minds. Hell, the ten of us knew what the other guys would do without so much as a look. In that first year of new recruits, we lost four; mostly because they were stupid, or we weren't watching out for them… I'm not sure which."

After taking a sip, George looked at the nine faces standing next to him. "Ya wanna see the only mention I've ever seen of the '*Lord's Leapers*'?"

In a chorus, the nine said, "Sure! Absolutely! Of course! Are you kidding?!"

George very carefully hobbled over to the back wall and stood under a framed newspaper that had a picture of all ten of the firefighters. All clean-cut, wearing Army-issue jumpsuits and helmets. Each carrying an ax, rake and old-style pump fire extinguisher on his back. The one-and-a-half-inch headline read, **"Ten Lords a Leaping! Bravest Blaze Battlers in the World!"**

"They messed up the name but, that's us. Actually, I like the "Ten Lord's a Leaping," chuckled George. Makes us sound like legends, like that old song, ya know… 'Leven blah

blah blah blah... Ten Lords a leaping..." he laughed and started coughing.

"How'd you get the name *"Lord's Leapers?"* asked the red-faced man.

George sat on the stool below the article. "When the newspaper reporter asked about where we'd learned to jump, we told him that we were trained in Britain. All us Yanks had been sent to do cleanup at the tail end of the war. But, as things go in the Army, somewhere along the line, the brass said we'd been picked to be a part of a coalition force and were to jump. So, we met up with our British counterpart, Lieutenant Lord Chauncey Beauchamp. He was not only in charge, but also our teacher. The reporter wanted a catchy title for the article, so he promoted all of us to British Lords. The name stuck. From then on, our moniker was 'Lord's Leapers.' There were ten of us when we got back to the good ol' US of A." George lifted his glass and drank the rest, then unsteadily walked back to the bar and asked for one more. "We'd meet up every year and drink a memory to those that left us in the battle. I'm all that's left.

George lifted his glass to the picture and whispered something, then finished off the glass and gently set it down on the bar upside-down.

"Hey George, I think you hit your magic number of nine with that last one," said Betty.

"I did," smiled George at her. "Well done mathematician."

"Okay George, one of us will drive you home," said Harry, looking back to see which one of his squad would have the honor.

"Nope. I can't do that yet," said George, lifting his glass back up and turning it over for the bartender to fill. "I got one more glass."

"Why one more?" asked Juan.

He looked at his last drink, number ten, sitting in front of him and picked it up, held it up, looking at it, inspecting it.

"So why number ten, George?" asked Brad.

"Cause," whispered George, taking a slight sip off of the top. "Cause I'm ninety-eight years old, tired of being without my friends, and…" he swallowed dryly. "I saw the doctor to-day—I'll be dead within three months." His eyes stayed trained on the glass.

"Come again?" asked Harry.

"By this time next year, I'll be pushing up daisies, and everybody will have forgotten about the *'Lord's Leapers'* or *'Ten Lords a Leaping.'*" He took a bigger sip.

The group stood in stunned silence looking from one to another, then back at George.

Harry was the first to lift his glass, followed by the other eight. "To George, and the other *'Ten Lords a Leaping.'* Your grit, your bravery, your trailblazing... We promise, you'll never be forgotten. Not as long as we're around."

The other firefighters chimed in, "Hear, hear! Well said! Absolutely!"

George turned to the nine, stood unsteadily, raised his glass in his left hand and saluted them with his right. All nine of the firefighters returned the salute. When George drank down number ten, the other nine followed suit, and all slowly put their glasses —open end down — on the bar.

►♦♦♦◄

Five years later, on the edge of the forest, just across the street from the Smokey's Bar and Grill, nine firefighters stood saluting a seven-foot engraved marble marker, each with a double Bushmills in their hand and their families standing behind them. On the stone were the ten names of the original 'Lord's Leapers' and their group picture, laser-etched in the hard rock.

"For George, our friend. By far, the bravest man we've ever met," said Harry. "May you, and all your comrades in arms, be forever remembered, as the 'Ten Lords a Leaping.'"

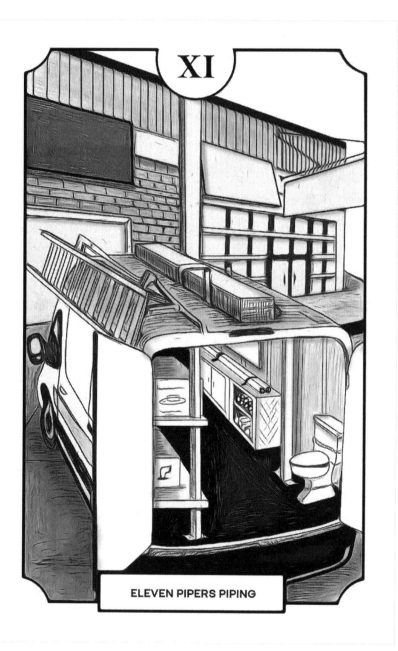

XI

ELEVEN PIPERS PIPING

Eleven Pipers Piping

PLOOF!

The last thing I remember was the light turning green. I had *Stairway to Heaven* blasting on the radio and was wondering to myself which grocery store would still be open at ten o'clock at night— I needed milk.

Then it happened…

PLOOF!

I was hit in the face by something. It broke my glasses and I think maybe my nose, I wasn't sure. I looked up and realized the airbag was cutting off my breathing. Somebody must've crashed into my eleven-year-old beast.

I did a quick run through. *Shoulder? Check.* Sore but not broken. *Neck?* Really, really sore, but I can move it so, *check.* Not broken. *Ribs?* "Ouch!" Okay so, there might be something broken there…

I put my hand up to where the handle's supposed to be on the car door and realize I'm now sitting in the passenger seat. "What the…" Before the words were out of my mouth there's this young kid, maybe twenty-two, to my right, yanking the door open.

"Oh man! Oh man! Don't be dead. Please, oh please… Don't be dead!"

"I'm not dead, but I *will kill* the…" I look up and smelled the kid before my eyes could actually focus on him. He smelled like he'd been doused in Wild Turkey inside and out.

I, of all people, would know. I've been in his shoes. "Let me guess, you were out with your buddies and you're late getting home." I tried to stand up, but my legs were too rubbery, so I fell forward.

"Oh man, oh man, oh man…" The kid held onto me and laid me back against what was left of the front end of my car. "Look Mr., I didn't mean it! I didn't see… That is, I didn't look… That is… It's…"

I put my hand to cut him off and he fell silent. "Look. I've been there, and I know what's going to happen. The cops are going to come, they'll take you away and charge you for what happened here. After that happens, and after you get out, come and see me."

I looked up at the kid's face. His eyes were wide, and tears were streaming down.

"After that happens, I want you to come and see me, got it? Come and find me." We could hear sirens coming fast behind us, getting louder by the second.

The kid seemed stone sober at this point. He was jumpy, his eyes were wide, and he'd agree to anything if he were offered a long rope to climb out of the hole he'd dug himself. "Charges! Charges! Oh man… This is, oh man, this is real."

"Yeah, it's about as real as it gets." I tried to take a deep breath, but I could only breathe a half a lung worth of air. Within ten minutes, four officers had the kid pinned to the hood of his car—what was left of it— and his hands were cuffed behind his back. Five minutes after that he was in the back of a squad car, and I was pulling away in an ambulance.

Three years after the accident, almost to the day, in comes this sullen, dark, curly-haired kid of maybe twenty-five, looking thirty-five. I'm sitting in my chair, going through the books. I looked into his coal black eyes that were like ice cubes, that is, when I was offered the chance to look into them. Most of the time he looked down at the ground. "Well, I'm here."

"Yes, you are!" I said with a big roar. "Now, you want to tell me who you are?"

The kid looked up at me like I grew a second head. I finally got a look in his eyes. I'd seen that look before. I saw it in the mirror when I was about his age.

"I'm Roger. The guy that... Well that accident about three years ago..." he tapered off.

"Oh! Right. Roger." Then I waited to hear what Roger wanted.

"You, uh... You said to come see you after everything was, you know, dealt with?"

"I did, did I?" remembering full well the conversation from that night three years before.

Roger shot a hard look at me and started to turn toward the door, "Yeah, well, if you don't remember, maybe…"

"Stop right there!" I barked. "You owe me! I didn't press charges; I can't help it the police and the judge saw it differently. It's okay that you spent time 'put away.' In fact, they probably cleaned you up."

Roger didn't say anything, he just looked back down at his shoes.

"Roger Dodger, I've been in your shoes. So, here's what's going to happen. The way I see it, you owe me for an old beat-up SUV, you owe me for the pain and injury of two broken ribs, and you owe me for three months off work. Now… do you have a job?"

Roger stared lightning bolts through his shoes and into the floor, finally shaking his head, "No."

"Well then, have you looked for a job, yet?"

Roger raised his face and the same laser beams were staring now at me. "Nobody wants to hire a con."

"Yeah, I remember those days." I went over to the corner of the room, picking up a dustpan and broom. "Here, take these. These will be your stock-in-trade for the next three weeks. After that, if you don't give me a lot of lip or guff, I'll start working you into the rotation. Any questions?"

The laser beams in Roger's eyes dulled to a light of inquisition. "Um, yeah, uh, what is it you do here?"

Half a year and over a thousand jobs later (I'm happy to say), Roger was fitting in nicely. He was at the shop every morning, 6 AM sharp. He yanked the old broken crap outta the truck, then restocked it for the day. After, he'd check the work order, to see what parts were needed, and he'd put them in. If we didn't have them, he'd improvise. He got really good at improvising.

Today, I've been working in plumbing for over forty years. I built up a six-truck business with ten other employees. Each and every one handpicked and trained by me.

Many, many moons ago, when I was a snot nosed kid, I was the apprentice to my father. My father was a hard-nosed, hard-drinking, hard-fighting, 'man's man.' He taught me to drink, and fight, and to have no couth. He taught me everything but compassion. That I had to learn on "the inside," as they say.

When I was twenty, I pulled the boneheaded move of straight away racing my old 1964 Chevy Impala down one of the local highways against an old Cutlass Supreme. It wasn't the race that got me in trouble. I'd been picked up for racing before. No, it was the half a bottle of Jack Daniels I drank before plowing into the farmer's manure pile. That got me three years with good behavior; which, of course I blew, and a really crappy night in lock-up—pun intended.

After I got clean in the clink, I realized I really wanted more from life. I was known in school as "Suck." I "sucked" at sports, "sucked" in class, "sucked" with girls, and *really* "sucked" in the relationship with my parents. The one saving grace was my old man. He "sucked" too. I won't say he took pity on me as much as he needed help, and he knew I was never going to be a neurosurgeon, rocket scientist, or preacher. So, when he met me at the jailhouse door, he drove me back to the shop, walked me into his office, handed me a broom and dustpan, and said, "Here, take these. These will be your tools for the next three weeks. After that, if you don't give me a lot of lip or guff, I'll start working you into the rotation. Any questions?" I've been doing it ever since.

After my old man died, my mom faded out, leaving me all alone. All she did really was watch the boob-tube and tell stories. I was never good about dating or caring about getting hitched. I really didn't know how to talk to women, let alone live with them. Besides the fact, being a plumber and pipefitter, well, you're on the road a lot. Sometimes, I'd have jobs out of town for weeks on end. Other times, I'd be stuck in town going from house to house and fixing toilets, putting in sinks, and replacing sewer lines. It's not the glorious job most women would want to hitch their star to. I mean, let's get serious, what woman wants a man that smells like raw sewage twenty-four/seven?

Mom used to take care of the books and scheduling. After she died, I ran the business by myself for about four years. I was happy as a clam but never had time to breathe. I worked seven days a week, twelve to fourteen hours a day,

three-hundred, and sixty-five days a year. Clogged toilets
don't care about Christmas, Easter, or New Year's.

Then it happened.

I had a cousin I was tight with growing up, Charlie. Well,
his kid, Timmy, had screwed up royally; hooked on coke and
every other kind of pill, powder, and liquid known to man. I
mean, this kid was a human dispensary. If you would've
freeze-dried his pee, you could've stocked an entire phar-
macy for a week.

Well, Timmy tried to find a job after getting out of the
'cleanup facility,' but nobody'd hire him. I mean *nobody*. He
tried to switch to a volunteer gig at the zoo cleaning up after
the elephants into a part-time job, he try to con the parks
department into letting him mow the parks, he even tried
getting a job shoveling after the horses at the stables... Nobody wanted to hire an ex-junkie. They were always afraid of
him relapsing.

So 'good ol' Cousin Charlie wrapped his arm around my
neck one Christmas Eve, handed me a Diet Coke, and said,
"So, you plumbers make bank, right?"

"Yeah, I guess so. I can pay the rent. Why?"

"Well, my little Timmy's having trouble finding a
paycheck. And I thought maybe..."

My reaction was immediate, "Whoa, whoa, whoa...
There is no way I'm taking on your problems."

Charlie looked like I had slapped him. His eyes went wide, his mouth went slack, and his face turned scarlet. "What you mean, '*problems?*' Timmy isn't a *problem!*"

"No?" I asked. "Then where is he? I'll tell you where he is. I just saw him out back with that dweeb, Petey, smoking a bowl. You need to touch him with your size thirteen boot, right where it'll do him some good, if you ask me."

Charlie turned scarlet again, then stark white, and sat down hard on the fireplace hearth. He just looked at the floor and shook his head from left to right slowly. A few seconds later, I realized he had tears coming out of his eyes and needed to blow his nose.

"Look, Charlie, I can't take anyone on unless they're clean. I mean *really clean*. Look, I did time in the clink. I can't touch alcohol, drugs, or anything else from now on. *And* I can't associate with people that do! You know that!"

Charlie just kept looking straight down. After what felt like forever, he took a deep breath and said the words that shot right through me. "That's why I came to you. You're like my brother. You're the only uncle Timmy's ever known. You got *clean*, clean. I thought maybe you could help my Timmy get clean and stay clean. You're the only success story of '*clean*' I know. And I sure don't want Timmy being like me. I mean, we all know what kinda screwup I am." Then, he started crying in earnest. It really freaked me out.

Two days later Timmy shows up at my office door at 6 AM. I looked out in the parking lot and there is his dad, sitting in the car with the engine running. "Hey Uncle Phil. So, uh, dad said you wanted to talk to me?"

"*Want* to talk to you? No. *Going* to talk to you…" I got a real evil grin on my face, "Oh yeah…" I handed him a broom and dustpan and said those immortal words, "Here, take these. These will be your tools for the next three weeks. After that, if you don't give me a lot of lip or guff, I'll start working you into the rotation. Any questions?"

"Aren't you gonna tell me how I've screwed up my life and how this is my last chance and all that stuff?" the kid said, looking the floor.

"Why? I took a slug of coffee. "You know you screwed up. I know you screwed up. Hell, the entire *world* knows you screwed up. Now, pull up your big boy pants and straighten out. Got me?"

He didn't say a word. He just stared at me for ten seconds, then went in the back and started sweeping.

Within three months Timmy not only had the shop spick-and-span but started stocking the truck and taking care of all the ordering for new parts, just like Roger. He took the time to research what the best mechanisms were and where we could find them for the best price. Then, he took everything one step farther and started doing the books for me. I mean really doing the books! I had no idea the kind of money I could be making! Timmy was the best thing that ever happened to the business! And me, if you gotta know.

But the part that makes me the proudest was Timmy stayed true to his word. Since Timmy's worked with me, he's never had another shot of bourbon, beer, or wine. He's never shot up, snorted, or tasted drugs again. For that matter, the guy won't even take aspirin! That's a little stupid but... there it is. He's dedicated to staying clean. Although, I think the whole vegan, tofu eating, Whole Paycheck thing is a little too far but, hey... The kid's a straight arrow so, who am I to complain?

I've gotta tell you, I've had a lot of kids—boys and girls—work for me over the years. One thing, most of the girls worked harder and stronger than the boys. Seriously! I've trained young gals to run pipe inside the walls of hundred and twenty-year-old houses and they did it quicker, cleaner, and better than some of the big, hulking, boneheaded guys. There was this one gal in particular, Jenny was her name.

Jenny was a quiet, big-natured, big-smiling, big-buxomed gal with burnt sienna skin and big hair from the wrong side of the tracks. She had a heart of gold that every idiot boy took advantage of from the time she was twelve years old. Her mother was from Kenya and father from Jamaica. The last time she saw her father was when he was stepping out on her mother with another woman. Her dad never came back, and her mom never forgave him—or Jenny.

Jenny's mom took out all of her personal problems on her. She'd had a bad day at work, it was Jenny's fault. If she drank too much, it was because Jenny was driving her crazy.

If she didn't come home for three nights and was out with some fly-by-night guy, it was because she didn't want to be tied down to Jenny anymore. As good-natured and golden hearted as Jenny was, she was damaged goods. She wouldn't get belligerently sloshing drunk, nor would she become fun and numb when she used. No. Jenny had learned how to be alone. Even in a room full of people getting high or getting trashed, Jenny was alone. She said the drugs and booze took the edge off of the feeling of being alone.

After she got out of detention and I gave Jenny the broom and dustpan, she quietly took them with no questions and just started cleaning. She zoomed right past the three weeks, and continued to clean in almost total silence, just asking for breaks and if there was anything else I needed, for the next two months. I'm not kidding, I barely heard a word from the girl. She didn't ask questions, she didn't make observations, she was just quiet. One day I came in at 7:15 in the morning and saw her sitting off in the corner on the stool with tears leaking down her face. I asked her, "Jenny! What's wrong? Why the tears?"

Instead of acknowledging anything, she simply wiped her face and just went back to work.

I walked over to her and held onto the broom. She turned her face away and wouldn't look at me. "Seriously, Jenny, what's wrong?"

A little squeaky voice came back, "Nothin."

"Niagara Falls ain't nothing. You got something! What's wrong!"

She let go to the broom and walked into the corner, nose practically buried in it. "Nothin, it's stupid, and I don't want to talk about it."

"Jenny, if it hurts you, it hurts me, and hurts the business. You don't want to hurt the business, do you?" I know, it was a stupid thing to say but... It's all I had.

Jenny finally stopped crying for second, dried her tears with her fists and barely whispered, "Today's my birthday..."

Yes, I am a total moron. I never looked at all the paperwork, I never looked at her address, I never looked at how old she was. I say again—I... am a total moron! Here's a young girl, in the beginning of her life, hard-working, completely giving, asking for nothing. And no one was giving her the dignity of actually *knowing* the one day we should be honoring her. I felt like crap. And I should have.

Thinking fast, I said (totally lying), "I know! I plan on taking you out to lunch today! You got something decent to change into?"

It took about 10 seconds for what I'd said to fully register. When it did, Jenny turned around, eyes still red and leaking, and she looked at me. "What?" was all she could whisper.

"You heard me!" I said too loudly, overcompensating my stupidity. "Have you got anything decent to wear? I plan on taking you out to lunch. Where would you like to go?"

She just stood there in the corner about twelve feet away, looking at me. She looked at the floor, she looked at her shoes, she looked back at me, then she looked down. "I... I don't really have anything nice."

I felt like a total idiot. "Well, how old are you?"

"I'm nineteen."

"Well then, happy birthday!" I said, "Looks like we have some shopping to do." I went back into the office and looked at what jobs I had for the rest of the day. I was supposed to replace a toilet, take care of five stopped-up sinks and sewer systems, and price out four new houses. I immediately got on the phone to the contractor and rescheduled the four houses for the next day. Then I called Timmy and three other kids I had picked up over the years and told them they would have to take care of the toilets and sinks. They were very happy to take on those jobs because they thought I trusted them. I let them think that. The real reason was I had a little girl who hadn't celebrated her birthday in *God knows* how long to take care of. Remember, I. Am. A. Moron! I should have thought of this sooner.

I walked back out into the shop and before I could say, "Let's go," there were two very strong and very soft arms wrapped around my neck with tears soaking through the left side of my shirt. Jenny was now sobbing. "Nobody... Nobody's ever taken me out to..." And the tears kept coming.

I hugged her back for about a minute and a half and finally said, "Here now. Let's get out of here before somebody comes in and sees us like this. They might think I care or something."

We had a great time! Well, that is, Jenny had a great time. I'm a typical guy. I walk into a women's dress shop and feel completely out of place. I don't know a thing about color, in-style, out-of-style, matching... nothing, nada, nope. All I know is for a hundred and fifty bucks, three dresses, two pairs of shoes, and a handbag, made a little nineteen-year-old girl feel cared about for a day. Ya gotta love Marshall's or Ross or whatever they're called.

When I asked her where she wanted to go to lunch, she had no idea. "I don't know... McD's"

"No freaking way!" I yelped. "If I'm out for lunch, I want to sit down and actually use silverware." Following through on my threat, we ended up at an upscale diner in the chichi part of town. It was an Italian diner with white tablecloths and a full place setting— fork, spoon, and knife. The water glass was already on the table and there was an empty glass for wine.

Jenny's eyes were the size of saucers as we walked in. She looked great! She had on a flowery dress that went past her knees and flat shoes. Before we left the store, she went into the bathroom and played with her hair, so she actually looked more like a woman than a girl. I almost didn't recognize her when she came out. All the 'tomboy' had been stripped off.

After we sat down and had a couple minutes to look at the menu I asked, "So, what'll you have?"

I looked over and Jenny had her lower lip curled in between her two teeth. She was gnawing on it, and it would slip out every once in a while. Her eyes were shifting from left to right and her little and ring finger of her right hand were bouncing on the table.

I asked her, "You, okay?"

She looked up at me with wide eyes and whispered, leaning into me, "Yeah, I think so. But, well…" Then she looked around the room.

"What's wrong? You can tell me."

"Well, it's like this… I've never really *been* in a real restaurant before. I'm not sure what I'm supposed to order."

And *that* was Jenny then. Today, she's a master plumber with a business degree from the local community college and is married to Antonio, another master plumber I picked up out of the streets and cleaned up many years ago. They have three rug rats at home and are working on the fourth.

▶◆◆◆◀

All totaled, I have ten of my "pipers." Each and every one of them somebody else threw away like old 1940s aluminum or, even older lead piping. Everybody's replaced their old galvanized and aluminum with copper and PVC. But for me, it's the old school stuff that means a lot. It showed real craftsmanship. To take something so fragile, so malleable, some-thing so possibly dangerous—and turn it into some-thing workable and a piece of art... Well, that's real mastery.

Today, I turned seventy-six, but that's not the important part. No. The important part is the unveiling. You see with Roger... that makes eleven of the twenty-seven or so throwa-ways I've taken in, dusted off, and got clean—eleven of them who stuck. Eleven souls that *might have* made something out of themselves on their own. Or not. I don't know. All I know is all eleven have made my life richer. Yes, they *all* were a pain in the ass, and still many times are. But they're my pain in the asses.

That's us. So, I may not be around much longer, but there's eleven good kids that didn't have a prayer, that now are part of a business, running it, responsible for it. But more importantly we're the family none of us ever thought we'd have. And *that* makes all the difference.

What the kids don't know is this— I went to a lawyer a few weeks ago and had some papers written up. I'm not get-ting any younger and neither are they. Between the eleven of them, there are eight spouses, twenty-three kids, and four-teen grandkids. No, none of them have my name, and none of them have my blood, but they all have my background. They all had a rough start, got knocked around, pushed around, and had the hard edges rounded off. They're all mine; but more importantly, I'm all theirs. One of these days, I'm going to wake up dead and there's still a business to run.

So, they don't know this yet, but overnight I had all of our trucks repainted. Yup, it cost me a pretty penny. And as of today, my seventy-sixth birthday, our company has a new name and eleven new owners. On the side of every one of our trucks, and on every one of our business cards, and on every bill, estimate, and website there's a new name…Eleven Pipers Piping.

XII

TWELVE DRUMMERS
DRUMMING

Twelve Drummers Drumming

Subject: Hello From Italy!

Peter R. <RebelWithAClue@H&H.com>

To: Sally R. <RideSallyRide@H&H.com>

Sept. 15 at 6:25PM

Hey Sis,

Sorry you and the folks had a blowout about religion. That sucks. I know when I moved out of the house (was that eight years ago? Geez!) their Bible beating was the main reason. If you need to, you know you can always crash at my place for a while.

I didn't have a chance to tell you before I left, but a week ago Gail came down with something and Jimmy asked if I'd fill her slot at the *Che Ci Sia Pace Terra Conferenza* (Let there be Peace on Earth Conference). So, three days ago I left for Assisi, Italy! Yeeeaaa!!! Lucky me! I'll be here for the next three weeks. I'm doing a retreat with a couple thousand people from all over the world, trying to figure out what it takes to find world peace. There's every religion I've ever heard of.

We have Indigenous peoples from a lot of countries, Wiccans, and good ol' "pedestrians in life," like me; all trying to figure out how to cut through the BS and find a baseline for peace. Hey! Should be easy, right? HA!!!

Today's Day Three, and I finally made it to St. Francis's tomb in the basement of the Basilica. No, it's not as ghoulish as it sounds. It's actually really cool! There's this... feeling you get, like all your cares leave as you go down the stairs and under the church. When you're with the bones of Saint Francis, all you feel is peace. I mean real peace. No worries sneaking in, no thinking about what's going on tomorrow, no "what did I forget?" none of that. You're just right there. When you come back up, the peace hangs with you, until eventually real life slaps you in the face. But, while you're down there... well, it's hard to explain.

OK, I'm gonna send this so you have it in the morning. I think we're what, seven hours apart? OH!! And can you send me a pair of earbuds? I forgot mine and good luck in finding a decent pair in Assisi! You know where my key is. I'll text you the address to send to.

All right, luv ya sis.

Give Peace a Chance.
The Coalition for Peace www.CFP@H&H.com

▶◆◆◆◀

Subject: Hello from Italy!
Peter R. <RebelWithAClue@H&H.com>

To: Sally R. <RideSallyRide@H&H.com>
Sept. 18 at 7:55AM

Hey Sis,

Sorry to hear about Mom and Dad being Catherine the Great and Attila the Hun. My advice—don't do what I did. Don't move out in a huff and get a coked-up roommate. Trust me, it blows (pun intended)! No. Try to stay on neutral subjects, and see if you can stay away from politics, religion, or dating. Those will all set them off. Trust me.

I've been here almost a week and can honestly say, most of this is crap. I mean, I've been on a LOT of these symposiums over the last six years with *The Coalition for Peace*, but this is a total bust. Everybody seems to have an agenda. But somebody's got to try. And hey, if they're going to pay for my trip, well… who am I to say no? But I am tired of being a part of the problem instead of the solution. That's why I decided to sign up with the Coalition for Peace.

Take last night. I met up with my friend Ahmad (who's an Imam from Nigeria), and Josef (a Druze from Cairo); we met at a symposium for world hunger in Kuala Lumpur a couple years ago. We spent the first two nights at dinner haggling about what heaven, paradise, whatever you want to call it—LOOKS like! Ahmad said it's a fancy garden. Josef thinks it's an oasis in the middle of nothing. The problem is NEITHER ONE will really LISTEN to the other guy's viewpoint. They don't know for sure, but don't tell them it could be something else or they'll blow up at you. It drives me crazy!

When they asked me, I told them honestly, I don't have any idea; and, in a big way, I'm not even sure there IS a heaven. Well, they acted like I was a serial killer! They both went off on me—spouting holy book babble that didn't mean a thing to me. I mean, I've read their books but, I don't know all the intricacies of what it means if the comma is before the word "light" or after it. I mean, these guys are really smart and normally think outside the box. But man, you question ANYTHING about what their holy writings say, and they go postal!

I don't know. Is it that we're taught certain ways when we're young and can't consider someone else might be right? I mean, it's not like anyone in Kansas City knows what it's like to grow up in Bangladesh, or Nairobi, or Auckland. Every society has its own ways, yet we judge them by OUR standards. What about THEIR standards? I don't have the concept down. All I know is, it's beginning to feel like a waste of time. But the food's amazing and so's the sightseeing. So, there is that.

OK, I'll wrap up. I'm going to 'The Music Corner.' It's a get-together where they play music to meditate to. So, we'll see if anything comes. I'm not into the whole, 'close your eyes and drift to your center,' thing but, I'll give it a try."

More later.

Give Peace a Chance.
The Coalition for Peace www.CFP@H&H.com

►◆◆◆◄

Subject: Hello From Italy!
Peter R. <RebelWithAClue@H&H.com>

To: Sally R. <RideSallyRide@H&H.com>
Sept. 21 at 1:46PM

Hey Sis,

Thanks for the earbuds! I love the cookies too. A taste of home.

WOW, the nuclear option! Damn! You've got guts. I never would have told them to back off, or you'll cut them outta your life! What brought that on??

My advice, cool down, go to work at the store, grab some extra hours, and show them you're an adult. Don't bring up that you think they're being "Cafeteria Christians," preaching one thing and doing another. Trust me, it really pisses them off. Did it. Done it. Ready to design a new tee-shirt.

I think the last time I wrote; I was going to 'The Music Corner.' Turns out it's more like the 'Music Coroner.' Zzzzzzz... They play weedy little tunes that never go anywhere. It's sooooo boring! Why can't it have a little life, a little spice? Christians always talk about the "Fire of the Holy Spirit." Well, this was a giant fire extinguisher.

I did finally get together with my buddy Jamil. He's a cool Hindu I met in New Delhi last year at the "Looking at Differences with Open Hearts" conference. We went to last night's meeting, *Finding Options in Personal Peace.* It was a bust, but we had a great time. He was into this Wiccan red head from Ireland sitting a row in front of us. When he introduced himself, he crashed and burned; it was hysterical! She actually asked him out for a burger!!! No joke! She asked a guy who reveres cattle as sacred out for a burger! Jamil's eyes about bugged out of his head and his mouth opened and closed about ten times, trying to come up with the words that would ask "Are you crazy?!" mixed with, "You're cute. Can I ask you out?" Well, you can see where that went! Never got off the ground.

Last night, Jamil took me to this great little vegan place over by Saint Clare's church and introduced me to two indigenous people. Let me explain. In the US, we call them "Indians," but in other countries like Australia and Brazil, Mexico, etc., they have different names. So, worldwide, any

"Original Peoples" are called Indigenous. Any way... One girl, Hanna, is from the outback of Australia, and the other guy, Herold, is from a reservation in New Mexico in the US. We got into a GREAT discussion about people being in tribes. I never thought about it like this before, but we ALL look for our own tribes. Think about it—people who love football, they have a tribe; people who work on Wall Street, they're a tribe; people who have the same political view, they have their own tribe. Well, Hanna and Harold were saying that when their tribe tries to communicate with another tribe, they leave the words out. Radical idea, huh?! They said that the way the ancients communicated was by sign language or symbols, so they didn't have to depend on words. That way there wasn't any confusion. It totally blew my mind! I haven't been able to stop thinking about it.

Another cool thing, most of the aboriginals have their own idea as to who and what made the world. But they don't get pent up about who's right. Like Hanna said, "It's not so important as to WHO or WHAT made the world, as it is they DID make it." Anyway, it's something to think about. Maybe meditate on? LOL— like THAT went so well!!!

Well, I'm taking the afternoon off and going hiking around the area. Hanna and Harold said it's a great way to clear your mind. And we BOTH know my mind is pretty cloudy. Who knows? I might end up in Rome! HA!

OK Sis, don't kill the parents. I'm too far away to bail you outta jail. Hee, hee, hee...

More later.

Give Peace a Chance.
The Coalition for Peace www.CFP@H&H.com

►♦♦♦◄

Subject: Hello From Italy!
Peter R. <RebelWithAClue@H&H.com>

To: Sally R. <RideSallyRide@H&H.com>
Sept. 23 at 10:21AM

Hey Sis,

I'm glad you and Mom are talking again. Don't worry, the old man will come around. Mom will have a talk with him, and he'll cool down.

So, the latest from here. Last night, this rabbi was talking about the word "reverence" in all kinds of holy writings. He said that the word "reverence" is one of the few words that shows up in almost EVERY sacred literature. It's in the Bible like seventy-nine times, the Koran nine; even some of the Wiccan writings have it. So, I'm going to spend a little time online this afternoon and try to figure out why.

In other news, after the hike and talking to Hanna and Harold over dinner, I went back to my room and put in my earbuds. For some reason, I drifted off to sleep listening to Native American chant with flute. It was that same group we heard when we were down at the Grand Canyon, when we were kids. I haven't listened to them in a while, so I put them on. I remember focusing on the drumming and dreaming of people from all around the world coming together—like the old Coke ad from the seventies, or the *We are the World* song. It was really awesome. Everybody got along, no fights, no yelling, and actual conversations. When I woke up, I couldn't stop smiling. It was the weirdest thing, I felt like I had no cares in the world. I know, it's soooo not me, right?

Anyway, Jamil, Hanna, Harold, and I are going to see the rabbi again and see what else he's got. So far, he's been the closest one to bringing people together.

More later.

Give Peace a Chance.
The Coalition for Peace www.CFP@H&H.com

►◆◆◆◄

Subject: Hello From Italy!
Peter R. <RebelWithAClue@H&H.com>

To: Sally R. <RideSallyRide@H&H.com>
Sept. 24 at 3:14AM

Hey Sis,

I know I just wrote yesterday but, it's three a.m., I've had WAY too much coffee, and I'm stoked! The rabbi we went to hear was a bust. He was making a lot of sense with some philosophy he was opening with, but when a really vocal Muslim started countering him with the Koran... well, it got bloody. No joke, the two of them went at it like a couple of roosters! So much for "peace!"

Anyway, Jamil and I went to hear a really old Franciscan who actually lives here at the Basilica and has since he was like fourteen. He's got to be in his eighties. It wasn't a sanctioned session. We heard from some other people in the dining hall, about this rad old Franciscan asking questions that mattered. He wasn't in a lecture hall. They said he was hanging in this field in the middle of an orchard, down below the Basilica, just sitting on a bench. When we got there, he had maybe twenty or so people listening. He was talking about the "general law of nature." It's the first time the ideas of "good" and "bad" actually made sense to me.

Basically, he said THINGS are not "good" or "bad," they just are. If something is used FULLY the way it's supposed to be used, it's considered "good." Every time. If the THING is not used for what it was made to do, then it runs the risk of being considered "bad." It's not ALWAYS "bad," but it doesn't live up to its full expectation? potential? of being TO-TALLY "good."

WILD!! RIGHT?! I mean, who's ever heard "good" and "bad" explained so easily before?

Oh, here's another one. He compared life, and all that we ACTIVELY do, as with MATH! I know, freaky, right? Just wait. He said, it's not the stuff we think about, or the stuff that just pops into our heads. No. It's the stuff we DO, that we act on. It goes like this:

Think of life and all our choices as a bunch of math formulas. If we decide to do the right thing, it's like two plus two equaling four; so, we're walking the path of "good." But if we make a little bit off decision—be a little "bad—" it's like two plus two equaling five. We're close to the right answer, but not 100% spot on. If we do something really evil, it's like two plus two equaling seventeen! Waaaaay off!

Here's the crazy part, there's no one to correct us! Well, not right now—no God, or Guru, or Boogie Man. Correction comes later, when everything is tallied up. Closest one to the correct answer goes to the next level of the game! OK, that was my take, anyway.

Now here's the mind-blowing part. If we keep making the bad decisions, we will be getting farther and farther away from the correct answer! He said all of us will make minor math errors in our lives. The key is to go back and "rework the math.". Yup, it's that simple. He said to trace the math back as far as you can to where you first started making mistakes, then change them. Basically, start from scratch. Every time you mess up, go back again. He said our lives always move forward, but we can make a choice at any time to go back and do the right thing. Just pull out the eraser and start over. The big thing is at the end of everything, those with the closest math, win.

OK, remember when I was running with Jimmy and George? I mean those guys were headed for trouble back in Jr. High! I started smoking weed with them after school and then we started hanging at the mall, trying to figure out how to rip off the drugstore. Well, it's sort of like that. I couldn't figure out why the teachers thought I was a bad kid. Then I realized that I made a left hand turn with the people I was hanging with. I backtracked and "found the right path," like the old Franciscan said, and I started over. Best early decision I made.

Hanna and Herold were there in the field with me, so were the Wiccan and Jamil. Hanna asked the Franciscan something about the Creator… I didn't catch the entire question, but he asked her a really simple question that I don't think any of us ever thought of before. He asked. "What religion was God?" By this time there were maybe fifty of us standing around, totally silent. Nobody had an answer. He smiled, pushing himself up off the bench, saying, "God didn't have a religion because he was God. Mankind needed a path, so he put a set of natural laws in every person's heart. That's why as long as our hearts beat, we are being asked by the Creator to do the right thing. Do the right math. That's why all of creation, every living being, starts with a heartbeat. It's God's way of giving us a rhythm to live by."

Like I said, mind blowing, right??? We all went back and sat around in the cantina and talked about what the old Franciscan said for the past three hours.

I just can't get it outta my mind. I'm not sure how this answers any of the questions about world peace. But I think there's something in there.

Anyway, I'm gonna crash for a couple hours. Let me know how the battle of Mom and Dad is going.

More Later.

Give Peace a Chance.
The Coalition for Peace www.CFP@H&H.com

▶◆◆◆◀

Subject: Hello From Italy!
Peter R. <RebelWithAClue@H&H.com>

To: Sally R. <RideSallyRide@H&H.com>
Sept. 26 at 8:51PM

Hey Sis,

I just saw your email and couldn't believe what I was reading. Uncle Edmond, dead. Wow. I don't know what to say. He was a great guy and the only person I know that could give Dad a run for his money.

I remember one time, Uncle E and Dad were going at it about something, and out of nowhere Uncle E YELLED at Dad, at the top of his lungs, "I LOVE YOU, you little shit!" Well, that stopped Dad in his tracks. He hemmed and hawed around for a minute until he finally said, "I love you, too." That was it. The battle of the silver-back gorillas was over. There was no winner or loser. I don't even think it was a draw. It just stopped right there. Like, they knew that whatever it was they were battling over didn't matter as much as them caring about each other. Kinda beautiful, sad, and weird, all at the same time.

Well, let me know when the funeral is and where. I should be flying back to the states on Oct. 5th.

More later.

Give Peace a Chance.
The Coalition for Peace www.CFP@H&H.com

▶◆◆◆◀

Subject: Hello From Italy!
Peter R. <RebelWithAClue@H&H.com>

To: Sally R. <RideSallyRide@H&H.com>
Sept. 27 at 2:32AM

Hey Sis,

A bunch of us went back down to the orchard below the Basilica again tonight and hoped to see the old Franciscan. He wasn't there, so a group of us just started talking about life experiences and tried to figure out "the math," like he was talking about.

Towards dark, a car stopped at the gate of the orchard. It was the old Franciscan! He saw all of us loitering out there and decided to stop and chat.

He asked us if we'd thought about the heartbeat leading to peace. We all looked at him like he grew a third head. I mean, how could a heartbeat create peace? Then he said he had to get up the hill but wanted us to think of one more thing. "When everything gets to be too much, always go back to the beginning." We asked, "Beginning of what?" He smiled, and said, "Of everything. Everything but God, Creator, World Builder—whatever you want to call them—has a beginning. Always go back and ask, what was this SUPPOSED to be, not what it turned into." And with that little brain teaser, he was gone in a cloud of dust. The twenty or so of us hung around for another couple hours hashing and rehashing everything he said, but we never came up with any answers for peace.

After we broke up, I went back to St. Francis's tomb. I don't know why, I guess I was kinda craving the same feeling of peace I found there the first week. I went down the steps, and again all the worries of the world stayed behind. It's like floating in a pool, totally buoyant, but still able to walk around. I just sat there, quiet, for the longest time. I didn't really think anything. I sure didn't pray. I gave that up a long time ago. I just sat there.

The longer I sat, the more things began to slip into my mind. I remembered the first big blowout with Mom and Dad about going to church. I remember the first big lie I told to my fourth-grade teacher. I remembered cheating on Judy when I went out with Becky. I mean ALL of it started flooding back. It's like the math thing, I was going back to all the places I made the first math errors. I should have felt like crap, but I didn't. I was still at peace. It was like I was seeing all my mistakes from the outside so I could judge for myself. And now, I can decide how to change things.

I don't really know how long I was there—all night for sure. I walked out the front doors of the Basilica as the sun was coming up. At breakfast, I ran into Reggie. He's a Southern Baptist guy I ran into down at the orchard. He said he had a weird restless night, too, and that the old Franciscan got under his skin. Reggie said he started "Going back to the beginning" on a lot of stuff. Come to find out, he's from New Orleans. He said, the best place for Cajun is *Mother's Restaurant*, and I need to try it the next time I'm down. The best part is he likes jazz! Big shock, I know. He said when he was a kid, he used to sit down in the Quarter with a couple buckets upside down and drum away on them for change. Now, he's a drummer in a jazz band and a second line. He told me he was going back to his room to catch a few winks, then meet up with a couple friends to check out a local band if I wanted to tag along.

So, I'll sign off now, get some sleep, and probably hook up with Reggie and his friends in a bit.

More later.

Give Peace a Chance.
The Coalition for Peace www.CFP@H&H.com

►♦♦♦◄

Subject: Hello From Italy!
Peter R. <RebelWithAClue@H&H.com>

To: Sally R. <RideSallyRide@H&H.com>
Sept. 29 at 2:12AM

Hey Sis,

I'm so sorry I can't make it back for Uncle E's funeral. I can't believe I'm going to say this, but I'll light a candle for him at the Basilica. No, I'm not going all holy roller, 'Praizzzz Jezzzus' on you! I just spent a few more hours down with St. Francis, trying to work through some stuff that kinda boiled up the last time I was there. I gotta admit, there's a certain... I don't know... reverence down there. Like there's a really thin veil between us and the souls on the other side of a curtain. It's sort of like time stops—no past and no future—only now.

Anyway, rambling...

And tell mom I lit a candle for Uncle E. That'll make her happy. I just found out almost all religions light candles or make fires in remembrance. It's like prayers rise up on the smoke. It's sorta beautiful.

Anyway, tell her I lit one.

Oh! Something else really cool happened last night. I went down to the orchard. I figured I could do some quiet thinking. When I got there, Hanna and Harold were already there and had a couple small ceremonial drums. They said the old Franciscan reminded them of something their tribes do. When the tribal leaders call on the Great Spirit for guidance, they set a steady tempo on the drums and just hold it there. Hanna said the nickname her elders gave it was "The Earth's heartbeat."

I didn't know where it would go but, I was willing to give it a shot. Hanna went to the East, and Harold West, I didn't have a drum, so I went to the South and just lightly clapped along. They set a perfect tempo, the speed of a heartbeat resting. What really freaked me out was when I checked my pulse in my neck, it was perfectly in sync with their beat!

We went on for a little over an hour out in the orchard. It was well past dark, and we didn't think anyone else was around. Out of nowhere, came a little higher pitched drum. Hanna and Harold kept going as the Wiccan (I found out her name was Rachel) played an Irish Bodhran that she'd brought along. After another half hour, we were all in our own little worlds. I was thinking about Mom and Dad and you, and all the fun we used to have together when we were younger. It was like all the BS of the world melted away; all that was left was the good stuff. The stuff that we'll all remember on our death beds. It was sort of like being down with St. Francis.

Well, long story short, we all agreed to meet back there tonight. So, I'm gonna sign off now and get some sleep. I did find an old snare drum in a pawn shop in town that I'm going to pick up later. So, we'll see if I still remember how to hold the sticks! HA!

Night Sis, miss you.

Give Peace a Chance.
The Coalition for Peace www.CFP@H&H.com

▶◆◆◆◀

Subject: Hello From Italy!
Peter R. <RebelWithAClue@H&H.com>

To: Sally R. <RideSallyRide@H&H.com>
Sept. 31 at 0:02AM

Hey Sis!

I—I really don't know where to start.

Tonight... OK—now its last night— was LIFE CHANG-ING! No, I'm not exaggerating! WOW!!! Where to start... OK... Hanna, Harold, Jamil, Me, Rachael, and some other people they told, all showed up in the orchard with drums. I went to the pawn shop and got the snare and went to the same clearing. We got there in late afternoon, so it was still full light.

Somebody must've told the old Franciscan what we were doing, because he was there, in his usual spot, sitting on the bench. It was really wild. We all came to him and gathered around. It was like something from another world—everyone sitting around the guru, or Aristotle or something, waiting for pearls of wisdom.

Well, we weren't disappointed! He didn't say anything for the longest time. He just looked at each of us and smiled. Eventually, he said, "You are here to find peace for the world, yes?" We all nodded. "But have you considered peace must come to YOU first? Each of you must find your OWN peace, here?" he pointed at his chest. "Here, within your own heart? Before you can make peace with your friends, you must find peace within yourself. AFTER your friends find their own peace, then you together can start to make peace with your family and wider friends. And after that," he shrugged "then you can go to your communities. But there must be peace within every single person along the way, otherwise a cancer begins to grow in the relationships. The math goes astray, all must be for the 'good' side of nature—not the 'bad' side—and it must be practiced daily, reverently. Only THEN will you start to BE the peace."

The old Franciscan got quiet and lowered his head. His eyes were closed, and he looked like he might be praying. There were twelve of us with drums of all different kinds—snare, ceremonial, conga, bodhram, damaru—you name it, we had it. We made a circle around the old Franciscan, everybody about ten feet apart, all looking into the circle. Hanna started and set a perfect heartbeat tempo, not too fast, just like a heart at rest. Then Rachael started, she was across from Hanna, after that we all joined in, very simply, all trying to feel the same beat Hanna had set.

I'll admit, it was rocky at first. I think all of us at some point tried to take over and be the leader. When that happened everything started going wonky, and we began to echo each other. But then, it clicked. We all gave in to the heartbeat. We locked in and, honest to God… I didn't feel like I was even playing anymore! I mean, my hands were there, they were on the sticks, they were moving, but I wasn't the one moving them! It was the heartbeat moving them.

Everyone in the circle was looking around at each other. The people sitting under the trees outside the circle were swaying back and forth and started to lightly clap their hands to the heartbeat. There was this... I don't know how to describe it... A feeling. No. More, an inner connection between all of us. It wasn't very strong, but it was there. Some people started crying, others giggling. It was like we all felt "It's gonna be OK. Everything happens for a reason. I'm here..." It's CRAZY, I know! It freaks me out writing it! But I swear, it TOTALLY happened!

Well, we all began to turn around, playing so we were facing out. We all just sort of acted as one, looking out, and sent the heartbeat out and away from us. I was facing straight West. The sun was going down, and the most vibrant colors filled the sky. I'd never seen such rich oranges and saturated golds and purples before. It was like I was seeing new hues. I lost it, I'm telling ya Sis, I bawled like a baby. But the entire time, I was smiling. It was like I KNEW peace and I KNEW there was something, somebody else out there that cared if I lived or died.

We played until about two hours ago, like six hours total. I gotta admit, we were all really sore by the time we finished, but none of us wanted to leave. We all stood around, smiling and giggling, and hugging and crying; not really saying anything. We didn't need to. We said all we needed in the heartbeat.

Needless to say, I'm too hyped to sleep, even though I'm waaaay pooped. I think I'll head downstairs and grab something to eat at the one and only all-night diner in town and try to process it all.

Well, that's all I got Sis. I just wanted to tell you that this has been an experience like I never expected. And I hope, and yes, I WILL say it—pray—you and I can heal whatever it is between us and Mom and Dad. I can see that peace really does have to start with me, like my new buddy, St. Frankie said.

Love ya Sis. Miss ya.

Give Peace a Chance.
The Coalition for Peace www.CFP@H&H.com

▶◆◆◆◀

Subject: Hello From Italy!
Peter R. <RebelWithAClue@H&H.com>

To: Sally R. <RideSallyRide@H&H.com>
Oct. 4 at 1:24AM

Hey Sis!

Well, this will probably be the last email before I come home. I'm sure you found out I called Mom and Dad yesterday. I couldn't NOT talk to them anymore. The Heart-beat circle has worked on me.

Since my last email, the twelve of us have gotten together just before sundown every evening and drummed well into the morning. Some pretty freaky and really mystical stuff started to happen. We all started to... I'm not sure what to call it... meditate on? think about? pray about? certain things.

The old Franciscan met us before we started playing and asked us to keep a boy in our thoughts as we played the heart-beat. He said there was this little four-year-old boy in Assisi who was hit by a car while playing in the park the other day and was in pretty bad shape. No one, especially the doctors thought he'd make it. Well, he asked us to, again, I'm not sure what the right term should be... I'll say pray (for lack of a better word) for complete healing.

Hanna took a deep breath and played a little slower, a little more thought-filled than before. It felt right. The surge came, and we were in sync, all thinking of the little boy. Feeling the pain and suffering of him and his parents. I opened my eyes and noticed everyone had tears running down their faces. I closed them again and saw a bunch of flashes—his blood slowing down, his brain shrinking, the breaks and cracks in is bones mending. We felt his heart rate pick up; and we all realized, our drumming had sped up to match his heartbeat! All of us! We just felt it!

We continued to play till early yesterday morning. Later in the afternoon, the old Franciscan told us the little boy was released from the hospital! He had to wear a cast on both legs for a while, but he was fine! Nothing wrong with him! The doctors couldn't figure it out.

Last evening, the old Franciscan sat on the bench and said he had only one more thing to tell us. "Tomorrow is the feast day of our Patron, St. Francis. He was born a sinner, living a sinful life. But he went back and redid his math. He went back to the beginning, finding humility and truth, using things as they were to be used—in their best "good" way. You don't need to drum to find peace. That is how YOU'VE found a small pocket to create peace for yourselves. You will leave soon. I hope you all find your own peace, first. Because it's in finding your own peace you'll be able to give it to others." He then looked at each of us twelve again, smiling, and said, "Now go, play the heartbeat for your OWN peace."

Word got out. There were maybe three or four hundred in the Franciscan orchard. The twelve of us made our circle, and Hanna started us out, the others clapping quietly. After sundown, we were in the zone. When we turned out from the circle. I saw you, and Mom, and Dad, all standing right there with me. I saw both grandmas and grandpas, and other relatives I'd never met. I saw and felt everyone's heartbeat, and the love that they had for each other. I stayed with that for a long, long time. It was magical. It was real peace.

When we stopped, we all turned back into the circle. The old Franciscan was gone! He'd disappeared! No one saw him leave. We asked. He was just *poof* gone. I can't explain it but, we all actually found peace through him. I'm still not fully sure how to get it out to the world, but it will come. Conferences? Meet-ups? A new movement? With time, it will come.

Well Sis, we celebrate St. Francis's Feast Day tomorrow… check that, later today! It's like 1 AM. And then I'm on a plane for home.

Oh! I almost forgot to tell you! When I talked to Mom and Dad, we leveled with each other. I told them I'd finally found a bit of peace over here and I really wanted to work things out with them. I'll be honest, I'm a little scared of how we're gonna make it happen. I don't know how to tell them they're being too pushy and that they need to back off a bit. But it will come. I now have faith.

Love ya Sis and can't WAIT to throw my arms around you and tell you, "I love you" in person. See ya at the airport.

Give Peace a Chance.
The Coalition for Peace www.CFP@H&H.com

►◆◆◆◄

Dear Petey,

I can't believe it's been a year since you told me about this place. It's exactly like you said. Today's October 4th and I'm here with Mom and Dad in Assisi. We met your old Franciscan when we got here. He told us about the talk you two had right before you left; that you were going to do everything you could to patch things up with Mom and Dad. He said you found real peace for the first time and wanted more than anything to share it with your family. With us.

And he told us about finding you and your eleven drumming friends after the driver lost control of the shuttle van, and that you and the others are in their prayers here in Assisi. He said you will be in their prayers from now on every St. Francis Feast Day.

I can't believe you're dead. I mean, it's just not fair. You were coming back to us. To me. We were going to be a family again.

Mom, Dad, and I came because the Franciscans are naming the field in the middle of the orchard the *TWELVE DRUMMERS DRUMMING PEACE FIELD,* in honor of you and your friends. The old Franciscan said we should each write a letter to drop into a little fire they were going to make in the middle of the field, by an old bench. He said we should write to you all we're feeling and what we didn't have a chance to say before... well, before you died. I know you lit a candle for Uncle E. I just hope the smoke brings my letter to you.

I love you. God, I miss you! And even though I DON'T want to let you go, I'm really glad you finally found your peace.

Your little sis,

Sally

Afterword

I first learned of *True Love* in the most casual of ways, the meeting of an author over lunch at Frisco's Barroom in the university-town of Webster Groves near the Opera Theatre of St. Louis, Missouri, where the very first reader, indeed the one for whom these stories were written, was serving as stage manager over a production of Mozart's *The Magic Flute*. It was in that encounter that the restaurant's back patio transformed into a tapestry of dialogue about ancient and modern-day saints and our capacity to cooperate with the grace God freely provides.

My throwaway question, "What's next?", which I often use as an exit strategy as my time with an author begins to come to its end, renewed the encounter. Who is this man, I wondered, who speaks so eloquently of all things great and small, of the greatness and smallness of humanity, and of how through grace our smallness is our strength?

In this work, author Benjamin Bongers captures the indomitable nature of our human spirit and invites his readers into the sublime. Like O. Henry's "Gift of the Magi," in which a young husband and wife of little means find creative ways to share their gifts with one another, Bongers' *True Love*, a joyfully tearful collection of short stories he wrote for his wife over twelve Christmases, evokes within its readers an empowering gasp of faith, hope, and love. This work does more than move the reader; it elevates the reader's soul.

This book, I believe, is the kind of classic that will endure for a long time and awaken all of its readers to the kind of persons that they are designed to be.

—Dr. Sebastian Mahfood, OP

September 17, 2022

Feast of the Sacred Stigmata of St. Francis of Assisi

Made in the USA
Las Vegas, NV
17 November 2022

59712739R00142